Doorways to the Unseen 4

6 Tales of Terror and Suspense

James Dermond

Ambages Books

Copyright © 2022 Ambages Books

ISBN 978-1-946038-03-6

Cover art by Jeff Purnawan

"When the woods are black as night, that's the Boogeyman's delight. Better run away, better run away, pretty little maiden, better run away!"

- Author Unknown

Contents

Fear of the Dark

"Nyctophobia, or an abnormal fear of the darkness. I've treated many patients with this condition before."

Susan could feel her heart pounding in her chest as Dr. Schreiber spoke, his monotonous, thickly accented voice gauzy and distant. The loud thumping ringing in Susan's ears drowned out any other sound in the room, deadening the doctor's words as he offered his diagnosis. She struggled to regain her breath as she lay on the office couch.

"It's common as a mild disorder in children, but this kind of psychosis will most often disappear before adulthood. In your case, however," the doctor said, his voice darkening, "the disorder has not only persisted, it's become more acute. That's quite unusual."

Susan could barely nod. What had seized her was the sudden resurgence of a childhood memory: she had been relating her previous anxiety attacks to Dr. Schreiber, when this particular memory—deeper, more visceral than the others—had paralyzed her. Dr. Schreiber hadn't seemed to notice.

Her breathing now once again slow and steady, Susan glanced obliquely at Dr. Schreiber. "You've just told me what my last therapist told me: that I should have grown out of this by now. But I haven't. It's only gotten worse, as you said. Much worse." Susan's voice was grating; she was irritated that

Dr. Schreiber had stated what she believed was the obvious. "I had to take a leave of absence from work this time, which is why I'm back in therapy. I explained all of this to your assistant over the phone."

Dr. Schreiber didn't immediately answer. Instead, he adjusted his reading glasses and flipped distractedly through several sheets of paper enclosed in a manila folder. Susan sat up, brushed her hair out of her face, and gazed directly at Dr. Schreiber. "Nothing's worked long-term," she insisted, hunched over at the couch's edge. "And I don't want to go back on medication either. The last prescription drug I took wrecked my concentration. I develop software applications and I need to be able to focus for hours at a time on lines of code. It's what I do most days."

"Ms. Neumann, please lie back down," Dr. Schreiber said finally, his inflection pronounced, masking a hint of frustration. "Our session isn't over quite yet. I'm still building your patient profile for future sessions, that's all."

This was their first session together. Susan had reluctantly agreed to contact Dr. Schreiber after her near-collapse last month; he'd come recommended by her brother, Peter. For the past few years, Susan had thought her fears were almost behind her—and then she'd experienced one of the worst anxiety attacks of her life.

Susan had described her most recent attack, which had put her temporarily out of work, to Dr. Schreiber. When he asked when her phobia had first taken hold, Susan began to tell him about the incidents in her recent past before touching upon the more dramatic attacks that had plagued her during childhood. Susan had always been afraid of the dark, for as long as she could remember.

Reclining on the chaise longue, Susan did as Dr. Schreiber had asked her. She placed her hands at her sides and rested her head on the heavy cushions against the couch's rolled

2

arm. Dr. Schreiber put a hand over his brow and closed his eyes tightly for a moment.

"Now, please, resume where you paused before I interrupted. I apologize for that; I should've let you continue," Dr. Schreiber said contritely as he reviewed his session notes, turning over a scribbled page. "Your worst attack before this most recent one occurred when you were twelve years of age," Dr. Schreiber stated, reading aloud, his voice again flat and monotonal. "Your parents had left you at home alone. They had gone out for an evening and there was an unexpected blackout."

Susan felt a shortness of breath come over her as the memory crept into her mind again.

Dr. Schreiber continued reading: "Your parents found you unconscious on your bedroom floor. The power company later said the outage had lasted less than an hour. Can you recall what happened during that time? Or did you faint as soon as the lights went out?"

"Dr. Schreiber, I want to stop for today, if that's all right with you," Susan replied hastily. She had buried the unspecified trauma deep in her mind's recesses, just she had trained herself to do. Glancing at her wristwatch, Susan hid a short gasp and sat up on the couch. "We're at the end of the hour I paid for anyway," she noted as she exhaled, her breathing gradually slowing, "and I have to get home before it gets dark."

"All right, let's stop here," Dr. Schreiber said amiably as he put aside his notes and reached for a different notepad, more relaxed now that the session was over. "I'm writing a prescription for you to help prevent another attack. I know you're reluctant to go back on medication, but these pills should have few adverse effects. Please make sure it's filled before we see each other again next week."

Susan gave Dr. Schreiber a terse thank you, taking her prescription note in hand. She left the good doctor's densely packed office, its shelves lined with medical books and curios collected from his travels. Picking up her bag from the clinic's receptionist, Susan passed a door plaque that read, "Dr. Hans Schreiber MD, PsyD."

The glass turnstile whisked open as Susan exited the building, hurrying toward her car left on a side street nearby. After hours, the parking lot was mostly empty now.

What kind of psychiatrist is he, anyway? Susan thought ruefully. *The poor man didn't even notice I was about to have another attack right there on his couch.*

Light snow was falling, and Susan knew it would be dark soon. She couldn't risk being outside at night so soon after her attack; she might have another crippling episode like the one she'd had in the underground garage at work. *About another hour of daylight left,* Susan calculated. *Enough time to get home if I'm alert on the highway.*

Fumbling with her car keys in the cold, Susan opened the driver-side door and took her seat behind the steering wheel. She exhaled and then breathed in deeply, a tightness having gripped her chest as the winter sun hovered above the tree line. It was a long drive to the suburbs, but Susan would be home before the darkness came over her.

The sedan's headlights beamed as she turned the ignition, flooding the empty two-lane street. Susan took another deep breath, the windshield wipers brushing snow aside, and then slowly rolled her car away from the curb and toward the traffic light ahead.

Susan turned off the street and onto the interstate highway, eventually exiting to the main boulevard of her residential town. She drove past small shops and restaurants and then down the quiet avenue where she lived, her home part of a scattered cluster of quaint colonial-style houses. The living room lights were on, as they always were when Susan left. She couldn't come home to a dark house, not ever.

Unlocking the front door beneath bright porch lights, Susan reached inside to flip an interior switch. She then went through her after-work ritual of heating a meal from the refrigerator, checking her messages on her phone, and finally sitting down to eat dinner at the kitchen table. *I still have so much to do*, she thought, feeling stressed. *I'm not sure when I'll get to bed.*

There was a new pop-up from her desktop messaging application: a message from Peter. Below a hyperlink was a message requesting that Susan join a video call as soon as she was able. Susan opened the privacy shutter on her computer's webcam and launched the video session with two clicks. Peter connected immediately.

"So, how's my baby sister?" Peter said, smiling genially from his desk chair, the room behind him lined with bookshelves and wall photos. Susan had spoken to Peter only once since coming home from the hospital last month.

"I just got back from my first session with Dr. Schreiber," Susan said, trying to hide her listlessness—she didn't want Peter to worry. "We talked for about an hour. He uses that corny Freudian couch method! I told him about my most recent attack and he put me on new anti-anxiety meds."

"Which ones? You know that some are addictive, right? I don't want you becoming an opioid junkie." Peter was half-smiling when he said this, but his eyes showed he was serious.

Reaching into her pants pocket, Susan took out a slip of paper and briefly examined it. "I'm not sure. I can't quite read his writing. I'm not a pharmacist, anyway. It's all Greek to me, as they say." Susan put the paper back into her pocket.

"Hard to spell and harder to pronounce: the brand names for drugs just keep getting weirder. But once you fill it, message me its name. I'll look it up and find out if there're any side effects. I'm worried about you, as always." Peter gave a pursed smile, his eyes sad rather than merely concerned.

"Don't be, Peter. I'm a big girl and I'll get through this like I always do. I can't miss any more work. My career can only be derailed so many times before it's over." Susan brightened, pushing her hair out of her face, and trying to reassure Peter with a smirk. "If software development wasn't full of manic depressives, I'd probably be out of a job already." She shot Peter a wide grin, her teeth finally showing.

Peter laughed, caught off guard for a moment by the uncharacteristic joke. "I think you'll be OK," he replied amicably, his anxious mood disappearing. "Dr. Schreiber came highly recommended to me through friends. Like you said, he's very old school, with the couch and everything. He might even suggest exposure therapy after more sessions: gradually getting you used to being alone in dark rooms."

Susan tried to hide her sudden shortness of breath, but Peter seemed to notice. He quickly steered the conversation in another direction, becoming livelier as if bestowed with sudden inspiration.

"You know, Dad told us a really harrowing story about our great-grandfather, Karl, when me and Hannah were kids. You were just a toddler at the time, so you never heard it." Peter looked away from his webcam and coughed.

"Now that I think of it, you didn't like being left in your crib at night, even back then. Mom had to put you in their room to get you to go to sleep. It's like you were always afraid to be alone in the dark, even as a baby." After mentioning this, Peter smiled apologetically—Susan knew he wanted to avoid further discussion of their mother. She was surprised he'd brought up their now estranged parents.

"Dad said Karl told him this story about something that happened to him when he was just a boy in the old country, before he immigrated." Peter sat up and leaned toward his webcam, the top of his head becoming large for a moment as he found a comfortable position on his seat.

"He had a terrible fear of rats; today, it'd be called a phobia," Peter continued, slipping comfortably into the story. "The Allies were still running their blockade after the war ended, so people were starving, especially out in the countryside.

"Our great-great-grandfather had died in action on the front, and Great-Great-Grandma Else now had ten kids to feed by herself. Karl and the other kids resorted to eating roots they had dug up from the forest, even the bark from trees. It was crazy.

"So, one day, he broke into a barn, mad with hunger. There was animal feed in the bins even though no livestock were left. Karl wanted to scoop up the feed for himself and the other kids, but rats were gnawing away inside the bins.

"Dad told us that Karl wanted to run screaming, but starvation got the better of him. Picking up a muck fork from the ground, he bashed the rats, spearing two of them with its rusty prongs. The rats shrieked, leaping from the bins and scattering.

"Instead of eating the feed, Great-Granddad built a fire, skinned and gutted the rats, and then roasted them right there on a spit. It was the first meat he had eaten in months, probably longer. After that, he was never afraid of rats, ever again."

Susan had been listening to Peter's story without comment. Now, she said disagreeably, "I'd rather stay rat-phobic. Or maybe starve to death instead. Why did you tell me that awful story?"

Peter leaned back in his chair and steadily gazed into the webcam. "To show you to face your fear. Nothing's as scary as it first seems. Maybe it could work with your fear of the dark, too?"

"I almost swallowed my tongue during the last attack," Susan said uncomfortably, looking away from her webcam. "Maintenance didn't tell anyone staying late that the lights had gone out in our building's underground parking garage. I stepped through the elevator door into total darkness, and that's when I seized up. There's no way I would risk an incident like that again, even for the chance of a cure."

"Well, just see how therapy with Dr. Schreiber goes. He's made real progress with others in your situation," Peter said encouragingly. "And always keep your meds with you once you get them. I'll message you again after next week's session. Night, night, baby sis."

Peter disconnected. Susan sat back in her desk chair, anxious, unwilling to move after the repulsive story Peter had told her.

Her older brother had been her rock these last years; he was the only family member she spoke to with regularity and she knew she could confide in him. What was strange was that, because he lived so far away, she hadn't seen him in person in years. Susan had slowly adjusted to a life with a steady job and without a therapist due in part to Peter's support; it was odd to think that throughout that whole period he'd been just a face on a screen.

Eventually bringing up a browser and signing into her work email, Susan sorted through her recent messages. It'd be a while before she was relaxed enough to attempt sleep.

Susan opened her laptop and scanned the weather report from an open browser. The daytime would carry on being cloudy and gray, but there was heavy snow forecast for the evening; it might be difficult getting home if she didn't leave the office on time. *I'll only be able to stay an hour over at most. More working at home tonight, I suppose*, thought Susan, sighing resignedly.

Peeking over her cubicle, she watched her supervisor, Isaac, duck into a conference room. He briefly made eye contact at the conference room door, a disapproving scowl on his face. Susan's report on the quarterly development project was due within the next week. Before her breakdown, she had missed a major development deadline. Irate, Isaac had reprimanded her in front of the entire team.

The cafeteria was busy; few people had left the campus for their lunch break. Snow flurries swirled outside the wide glass window next to Susan's table as she ate her salad on a tray, the steady din of conversation surrounding her. On top of the nighttime dark, overcast days and stormy weather often put her off, affecting her spirits. Thunderstorms reminded her of that night when her parents had left her alone in the house for the first time, the night she'd tried to explain to Dr. Schreiber . . .

"We'll only be gone for a while, Susie. Just long enough for dinner and a movie. You're old enough to stay home by yourself now. You'll just have to get used to it." Susan's mother stood over her, touching her hair with a reassuring smile.

Susan stared back at her mother with a worried expression, saying nothing.

"You'll be starting high school next year. No more baby stuff from now on."

Susan watched from the window as her parents' car backed out of the driveway and disappeared. A thin film of rainwater coated the glass, distorting the image of the moving car and the trees in their yard. Susan's parents had planned this evening weeks ago, so the bad weather hadn't deterred them.

Alone now, the last light of the day faded through the window as storm clouds gathered. Susan turned on the lights in the kitchen and living room before going upstairs to her bedroom. By the time she'd made it to the bedroom light switch, the hallway had become dark enough to make her nervous.

Sitting at her desk, Susan reached for her homework but then paused, feeling an uneasiness as distant thunder rumbled outside. She opened the desk's bottom drawer and took out a sketchpad, flipping it open to a page in its middle.

On the page was a sketch of an old house from the turn of the century, perhaps earlier. The pages of her sketchpad were filled with pictures of houses, flowers, horses, and other subjects, but this house seemed to Susan to be a recollection of some sort: something she had seen before but couldn't place. There were other things at the edge of Susan's memory, things that frightened her, so she hadn't dared draw them.

Taking a charcoal pencil from its set, Susan began to fill in the shading across the old house's roof, darkening its arches and coloring its shingles. The backdrop to the house was mostly barren: just the beginnings of leafless trees and thorny bushes that quickly faded into smudges.

Thunder cracked and boomed abruptly, and a torrential rain began to pour, rhythmically beating down against the side of the house. The curtains to her bedroom window were closed, but Susan could see flashes of lightning through the sheer material.

Susan stood and saw that her closet door was open. Mom must have opened it before she left, she thought, as she always made sure to keep it shut herself. Susan had only taken a single step when the room went black. Her desk lamp's lightbulb and bedroom ceiling's light fixture sputtered, their filaments sizzling into nothing.

An intense fear washed over Susan, her breath becoming jagged and frantic. She blindly stumbled forward in the dark and stubbed her foot against the bed, her terror mounting with each passing moment. A slow, ominous creaking came from behind Susan. It sounded like ... the closet door opening ...

The snowstorm was worse than the weather forecast had predicted. Susan drove cautiously home, having left work early. Isaac had watched her walk out the door, not saying anything but wearing another disapproving scowl on his face. Susan had been taking her newly prescribed medication—it was likely why she hadn't had a full-blown attack when the memory of that night had wormed its way into her mind.

The porch lights shone brightly, illuminating her snow-covered home and the buried front steps. Susan hurried inside, turning on a standing lamp near the door and then switching on the hall light. She hurried upstairs to her home office and sank into her desk chair. Another meeting invitation popped up on her computer.

"Peter! How are you? Why did you message me before my next session?" Susan tried to seem cheery, but she was still agitated after what had happened at lunch.

Peter stared silently into his webcam for a moment. Finally, he sighed. "I was just worried about you. Something told me to check on you before your next appointment with Dr. Schreiber. Are you feeling any better with those meds you're on now?"

"Ah, much better, in fact. I haven't felt this steady in a while." Susan didn't want to tell Peter about how close she'd come to an attack in the cafeteria. "Nothing to note, otherwise. Big project at work; I'll have to get to that soon, so I can't talk for long." Susan flashed a perfunctory smile, attempting to put Peter at ease.

"My sister, always the workaholic. Mom and I thought you would be an artist when you grew up. You loved drawing when we were kids." Again, Peter appeared ill at ease after bringing up their mother.

Susan stopped smiling, her tone now more somber. "It's something I just drifted away from. I'm not sure entirely why

11

it happened. I outgrew it, along with other things. Probably because I didn't see a real job in art."

"There's something else I wanted to mention too: Dad told us another story about Great-Granddad. One even scarier than the one about the roasted rats." Peter watched Susan through his webcam as if assessing her.

"And you're going to tell me this one whether I want to hear it or not, right?" Susan looked away from her webcam and turned to the open door behind her. The hallway light was still on.

Restless for a moment, Peter shifted in his seat. "The story came back to me after I told you the rat story. It's funny; I hadn't thought of it in so long, which is strange as it's 'out there' to say the least. Would you like to hear it?"

"So, what is it? Was Karl still back in the old country when it happened, whatever it is?" Susan was intrigued now, even though she could sense that Peter was subtly probing her, his reasons unclear.

"Dad told us that after eating the rats, things didn't get much better for Karl. Food stayed scarce, and Else had to put some of the kids in an orphanage.

"As he was the oldest boy in the family, Karl was sent away with several of his youngest siblings so he could keep them safe. The orphanage was packed with children who had lost both parents during the war and other kids whose families couldn't feed them. The nuns had converted spare rooms into sleeping quarters, with the kids more or less piled on top of one another.

"Their first night there, Karl was put into a room with his brothers and sisters and about a dozen other children. All of them slept on cots along the bare floor. The room had previously been a bedroom for staff but had been unused for years.

"Karl told Dad that a nun put them down to bed after leading their prayers and then took the only light in the room, a candle in its holder. Candles were in short supply, as was everything else.

"The bedroom's closet door had been left open, and Karl's cot was right next to it. The room was almost entirely dark, but he still couldn't sleep. He was so hungry it kept him awake.

"A clock chimed midnight in the distance and Karl heard a creaking sound as the closet door was pushed open wide from the inside. Karl swore to Dad that he saw a horrible thing emerge from that closet—it passed close to him but went by. It resembled a man, but was very bent and crooked, too tall and too thin to be a human being.

"The thing shambled forward, treading among the slumbering children until it reached the cot of a little girl who had been left all by herself at the orphanage. The thing scooped up the sleeping child and bundled her into a sack it carried before silently making its way back across the room.

"Great-Granddad wanted to scream but held it in, knowing what the monster might do if it heard him. He shut his eyes tight and tried not to move. He said he felt the thing come toward the closet and hesitate somewhere close by, as if it was looking down at him. Finally, though, the closet door creaked shut. Still, Karl didn't dare open his eyes until he could feel the morning light on them."

Susan breathed out at last. She'd been holding her breath without realizing it and now almost gasped, a shiver running down her spine. "Peter, why would you tell me a story like that?! You know the last thing I need to hear is a spooky tale about dark closets and child snatching."

Peter smiled slightly and then peered into his webcam. "I just wanted you to know that our great-grandad also had a terrible fear of the dark. Maybe it runs in our family."

"Did Karl claim he kept seeing this thing? What happened to the little girl?" Susan gulped.

"Dad told me that, after that, Karl would beg the nuns to leave a lit candle by the windowsill each night. He was so terrified of the dark that the nuns took pity on him. Each night thereafter, he would always make sure that the closet door was shut tight before the children went to sleep.

"As for the little girl, the nuns assumed she had run off in the night—this wasn't a rare occurrence at the orphanage. More children went missing before Karl and the other kids finally went home."

Sarah gasped, raising her hand to her mouth. "What did Karl say it was, this dreadful thing that steals children?" Susan didn't quite want to know.

"He said it was *'Der Schwarze Mann'*—a kind of shadow man from folk tales. We'd call it a boogeyman. He swears it was real, according to Dad. After moving out of the orphanage, and even later as a married father, Karl always slept with a lit candle and made sure the closet door was locked tight."

"Peter, I have work to do. If anything, telling me about this boogeyman has only made my anxiety worse. Please let me know if you have anything good to say instead." Susan reached into her laptop bag beside her chair, partially falling out of Peter's view.

"I do. I love you, little sis. I just want you to be well. And I just thought Great-Granddad's story might be worth retelling. You can mention it to Dr. Schreiber for analysis—he's from the old country too."

"So, you fainted immediately then?" Dr. Schreiber said while taking notes, pausing to give Susan a chance to reply. He'd thought that Susan appeared quite taut and strained when he met her outside his office; the medication he prescribed for her last week didn't seem to be working.

"Yes. I fell unconscious almost as soon as the lights went out. I didn't come around until Dad picked me up off the bedroom floor and started talking to me. I can't really remember what happened before that." Susan breathed weakly on the couch, feeling exhausted. "When they took me to the hospital that night, the doctors said I had gone into shock."

"And that's when you first developed your phobia? Before, you were fine in dark places?" Dr. Schreiber was becoming genuinely worried that Susan presented a much more serious clinical case than he had initially thought.

"No, I wasn't—I was always nervous about the dark. Mom would reluctantly keep my door ajar and a nightlight in my room while I slept. And because of my age, I was never really alone, especially at night. But, after the blackout, my fear became a terror." As the memory grew vivid, Susan rolled her head to one side, her breathing shallow. "I would sometimes start to panic just at the thought of dark nights, empty rooms with no lights, our basement, and so on. But worst of all was the idea that my bedroom closet door had been left open."

"Your closet door? Please let me know more about that. Was it because you fainted in your bedroom?" Dr. Schreiber coughed sharply, his uneasiness growing as Susan's story began to resemble that of other patients, also young adults, he had treated years ago. All had been deathly afraid of the doors to their bedroom closets, and all had refused to leave them open at night.

"I know it's unbelievable, Dr. Schreiber, but I swear something came into my room that night through my closet door. It took me somewhere but, somehow, I escaped. I think it wants me back now, after all these years." Susan sat up abruptly on the couch, her face drawn, her eyes beginning to bulge. Her voice quavered as she made a plea: "That this is real is impossible, but my instinct, or maybe my subconscious, tells me it's true. Help me before that black thing takes me away, this time forever."

Before speaking, Dr. Schreiber cleared his throat, a moment of mounting dread coming upon him before passing away. "Ms. Neumann, medical science, as well as my experience as a therapist, tell us this kind of acute phobia is rooted in a fear of abandonment, typically parental abandonment. There's nothing to fear in the dark, especially in your own bedroom. Subsequent sessions will reveal this once we discuss your earliest memories. Why, your—"

Susan stood and looked directly at Dr. Schreiber, suddenly calm. "Dr. Schreiber, I have to go. There's a winter storm alert. The snow should start coming down soon. I need to be on the road before then."

Dr. Schreiber glanced at the wall clock, noting the time. "That's fine. We can stop before the end of the scheduled session. I would have never let you go over, of course." He smiled, noting the dark, bluish circles under Susan's eyes and her spent posture. "Session three will help us find the underlying cause of this. I'll see you then."

The roads had become icy, so Susan drove slowly, closely watching nearby cars. Her car's windshield wipers squeaked, pushing aside the snow flurries that were quickly becoming thick snowfall. Night had come by the time Susan arrived home, and the lights of her front porch were obscured by the rising snowstorm. There were times when Susan couldn't tell what was real and unreal; she wondered if her new medication was to blame.

Susan settled in her desk chair and joined Peter's new video chat session. Peter looked worried today—it was as if he had anticipated what he saw through Susan's webcam.

"Hey, baby sis. Calling to check in on you. How did your session with Dr. Schreiber go?"

"I've packed my bags. I'm going to take another extended leave of absence from work. If they fire me, I don't care." Susan rubbed a blemish under her eye, its lid heavy from lack of sleep.

Peter's expression changed to one of surprise. "Why? You can't leave now. I thought you were getting better," he asked, a hint of desperation in his voice. "You might never work in your field again if you just drop out. You have to think of your future too. Where would you go?"

"Someplace sunny, far away from here. I don't care; I just need to go." Susan's mind seemed to have been made up.

Peter let out a weighty sigh and then folded his hands. "Let's talk about this before you make any rash decisions. You must stay in that house, Susie. Please, I'm just trying to help here."

"There's nothing to talk about. My fear of the dark is only getting worse, and a change of location might improve things for me. I'm planning on leaving tomorrow morning." Yawning, Susan began to reach for the shutter of her webcam as if to end the session.

Peter spoke hastily: "I did some research about *Der Schwarze Mann*. I had to auto-translate the sources I found online—there wasn't much in English."

"What did you find?" Susan asked, pausing for a moment.

"Folk tales about *Der Schwarze Mann* go back centuries, if not longer. According to folklore, *Der Schwarze Mann* puts the children he kidnaps in a sack and then takes them to his hideout in the space between worlds. If he somehow misses a child he tried to steal, or a child ever escapes, he'll stalk them forever, even menacing their children or their children's children. But he only ever steals children, never adults." Peter spoke as if he was reciting his source word-for-word.

"What happens to the adults he wants? The ones who escaped him when they were kids?" Susan was listening to Peter intently; the lore, she thought, might be more than just some dark fairytale.

"I don't know. The only way to stop *Der Schwarze Mann* is to lock your bedroom closet door and keep a light on while you sleep. He has all the time in the world, so he'll just keep trying. But once he's gotten a child in the family line he's been stalking, he'll move on to new children in other families." Peter scratched his head and made as if to say something else, but Susan interrupted him.

"Peter, the snow's going to start really coming down soon. I need to finish packing a few things. We can talk again tomorrow morning. Let's end this for the time being." Susan yawned again, hoping that sleep would come easily for once.

"All right," Peter said resignedly. "Check in with me early tomorrow morning. And don't call into work before we can talk this over. Is it a deal?" Peter smiled hopefully at Susan.

"It's a deal. Goodnight, Peter. I'll be fine. See you in the morning."

Peter made another smile, this one oddly curious, as Susan glanced away for a moment.

Closing her webcam lens, Susan powered down her computer. She stood and looked around her home office, surveying the items that still needed to be stowed into boxes. *I'm just going to bolt and then call Peter later. Getting through the plowed snow on the roads tomorrow shouldn't be a problem*, Susan thought.

Susan paused in the hallway. Her bedroom door was open. *There should only be a few more things I need to pack in here*, she thought, stepping into the room.

The lights went out. Susan stood totally still, listening. There was nothing except unfathomable blackness, the diffuse light of the moon outside blocked by the closed curtains.

Did I leave the closet open? Panicked and breathing hard, Susan rushed forward into the darkness, groping along the nearby wall toward the closet door at the room's far end.

Susan blinked. There was light, suddenly, albeit dim. She stood in a seemingly endless hallway, a row of wooden doors disappearing into infinity on either side. Susan swallowed and then squinted into the semi-dark beyond. An eerie yet dreamy glow seemed to be emanating from the flaking walls, the plaster crumbling around her.

Susan turned, finding nothing behind her except the hallway's vanishing point: an empty space from which the rows of doors began.

Taking a few steps down the hallway, Susan paused at the first door she came to. She slowly turned its antique knob and peeked inside.

A child lay on his bed, fast asleep. Toys and stuffed animals sat on shelves and a globe rested on a desk near the bed. The young boy turned in his slumber, as if disturbed by the sound of the door opening.

Quietly shutting the door to the child's room, Susan continued down the infinite hallway. She stopped at another decrepit and timeworn entryway. Soft, lamentable sobbing—that of a young girl, Susan thought—could be heard from the other side. The door looked familiar. Susan was afraid to open it.

Where am I? I've been here before, but how? Is this all a dream? But I never went to sleep! Real, tangible fear began to take hold of Susan, the onset of a severe anxiety attack building in her chest.

Susan bolted. She sprinted down the hallway, racing past door after door, her heart pounding, each breath biting into her heaving lungs. The gulf between her and the end of the hall seemed to grow wider as Susan ran, as if the hallway itself were being stretched at an almost impossible length.

Reaching the final door at the far end of the hall, Susan flung it open. She stepped into what appeared to be a large playroom full of broken dolls, stringless marionettes, and other castoff playthings strewn about its moldering floor. From the playroom's ceiling hung many sacks, their contents squirming and weeping.

Glancing upward, Susan crept carefully beneath the hanging sacks to the room's end. She made her way through the open door, a wide staircase suddenly descending before her. At the bottom of the stairs stood a once-grand but now dilapidated foyer, its chandelier dark and neglected.

A hoarse laugh echoed from somewhere behind Susan, then grew louder as if approaching her. The sour laugh gradually transformed into a deep and sinister crackle, which continued until the walls of the strange mansion began to shake, enveloping Susan in its ghastly mirth.

Rushing toward the wide double doors, Susan pulled at the ornate handle and disappeared into the tenebrous night outside. There was nothing around the mansion save for sickly, barren trees and thorny, lifeless thickets, a pervasive mist obscuring whatever spaces might exist beyond.

Mommy, Daddy, why did you leave me alone in the house that night? Peter, where are you? My closet door, she left it open! Blind panic frothing within her, Susan fought back tears. She ran on, staggering through the dreamlike dark.

A wooden door stood by itself not far away, oddly out of place in the empty field. An eerie phosphorescence beamed from under the door's sill. Susan stopped and turned to peer into the gloom: a wobbly figure was hobbling behind her, its features not visible, but as frightful in aspect as it was gaunt and misshapen.

Susan reached for the mysterious door's knob and stepped through its waiting threshold. Finding no footing as she exited, Susan found herself falling . . .

She tumbled down her home's long flight of stairs, her neck twisting and then snapping with a sickening crack. She died almost instantly.

From out of the darkness of Susan's bedroom reached a lank, emaciated hand, closing her closet door shut from the inside with a gentle click.

The Benefactor

"**Y**ou said you'd work the graveyard shift. That's why we hired you."

Daryl was filling out a stack of paperwork as his supervisor, Malcolm, spoke to him from behind his desk. Today was Daryl's first day at his new job.

Daryl had just been fired from his previous security job for suspected theft and hadn't had the luxury of being choosy about his next position. But this nearly derelict hospital—on the far side of the bridge, in a part of the city he would never have visited otherwise—had been willing to hire him right away.

An employment agency had connected Daryl with Malcolm earlier in the week. Yesterday, Malcolm asked Daryl over the phone to report to work in the early evening instead of at midnight so he'd have time to fill out the required forms and go over his duties. Malcolm had told Daryl he was never in the hospital building during the late-night shift, but that everyone who worked the shift reported to him.

"It's such a hard-to-fill vacancy. Well, that's everything. Just sign here and then here. You'll get your first paycheck mailed to the address on file in about two weeks." Malcolm tried to smile pleasantly as he watched Daryl complete the final form, but it was late and he wanted to be at home.

"Thank you, sir. I'm glad to be here," Daryl said with a modicum of sincerity. "I'm sure we'll have a good work relationship."

Malcolm rested his folded hands over his conspicuous paunch, not saying anything, but still smiling.

"OK. You can grab some dinner across the street at Melvin's—everybody who works late eats there, including the nurses." Malcolm's smile faded. "But we don't want any trouble with them, you hear me?"

"Yes, sir. I'll keep my hands to myself, sir," Daryl reassured his new boss, putting his pen back into his shirt pocket.

"That's good, that's good. If you work the graveyard shift, you won't see too many of 'em anyway. Besides, most of the pretty ones work during the day. The point is, don't get too friendly with the nurses." Malcolm stood and shook Daryl's hand, walking around his desk to see him out of his office.

"At least an hour before midnight, take the elevator to the thirteenth floor," Malcolm reminded him. "Look for Reggie and take over for him once he shows you the ropes. Otherwise, your shift starts at midnight every night you're scheduled unless I say different. I won't see you again for another few weeks—not until our monthly staff meeting on the last Thursday of the month."

Walking through one of the hospital's revolving glass turnstiles, Daryl exited onto the busy street. It was a warm summer evening, and he watched a hazy orange sun drift over the tops of the tall buildings on the borough's far side.

Daryl missed his hometown upstate, but he was excited to have moved to the city and eagerly anticipated the opportunities he believed it would eventually offer him. Would he gain fame one day as an actor? That was his hope.

Daryl explored the city blocks and then ate his dinner at Melvin's. Leaving the restaurant, he sprinted across the street to the hospital's main building, its floors now lit against the backdrop of the nighttime city. Daryl narrowly dodged the oncoming traffic, coming close to a speeding taxi. Reaching the hospital, he paused at the corner.

The corner was different from its companion at the hospital's front. It too was inlaid with gray bricks, but there was a dedication plaque, likely to a donor or the hospital's founder.

Examining the dedication, Daryl noted the hospital's name and a date late in the last century. There was also a man's name: Nathaniel Wingate. The dedication under Wingate's name read, "For our lives eternal." There was a circle in each of the plaque's four corners and within each were ornate symbols and letters, too small for Daryl to easily decipher.

Daryl walked through the hospital lobby and took an elevator to the thirteenth floor. A bell chimed as the elevator doors opened, allowing him a view of the floor's reception desk. Daryl greeted the nurse on duty as he approached and asked for Reggie, indicating that he was the new midnight shift guard.

"Reggie's finishing his rounds. He should be back soon," the nurse replied affably. "But there're still hours to go in his shift. Aren't you early?" The nurse seemed perplexed that anyone would want to get a head start on the graveyard shift, especially on the cancer and hospice floor. Daryl inhaled the faint smell of death, an odor even the antiseptic couldn't hide.

"Yes, but I didn't want to spend it in the downstairs lobby. Malcolm said I could show up early if I wanted to." Daryl looked around and saw there were still staff wandering the halls. He knew almost all of them would leave before he began his shift.

"Suit yourself. You can wait in the nurse's lounge down the hall until Reggie circles back. I made fresh coffee only an hour ago." The nurse gave a tight smile and turned back to the magazine she had previously been engrossed in.

The walls of the hospital looked worn and tired, as if every place Daryl went desperately needed a fresh coat of paint. The doors to the patient rooms were also shabby, with black adhesive tape placed over the odd inset window. Daryl wondered if anywhere in the hospital had been renovated recently.

He stopped at a wide picture window further down the hallway and peered out over the city. High-rises blocked most of the view of the bay, but Daryl could still see the body of water and a small island in the distance. The thirteenth was the hospital's top floor and, according to Malcolm, it would soon be nearly deserted.

Daryl pushed open the door to the lounge and found two nurses in conversation. Foam coffee cups in hand, the women turned as Daryl entered.

"You the new hire?" the younger nurse asked, emptying her cup and tossing it into a waste bin near the metal sink.

"Yes, ma'am. Today's my first day. On the night shift. I'm going to meet Reggie soon." Daryl tried to be polite, but the women seemed to be in on a joke that he wasn't aware of; the older nurse wore a sly grin as he replied to them.

"Well, good luck with that. Not many can handle the graveyard hour shift up here. Most quit after some months or even a few weeks. Some of the nurses think there's something 'off' about this floor." The younger nurse was smirking now, as if unable to believe that anyone would be foolish enough to take this job.

"You don't say. You mean like the floor is haunted or something?" Daryl didn't believe in the supernatural, but he noticed the nurses seemed serious, even convinced.

"Can't say," the younger nurse replied. "No one except the late-night shift guard ever sees anything. The guards sometimes complain that they see or hear things at night. Since I've been here, a few guards have just up and left without warning. Punch out at the ends of their shifts and don't show up for work the next day. Some don't even bother to call." The nurses exchanged glances and then walked past Daryl, not bothering to make any pleasantries as they exited the room.

Daryl stood alone in the lounge, thinking back to his phone call with Malcolm. Malcolm had asked personal questions—if he was married, and if he had any family in the city. No, Daryl had told him, he was single, and his parents weren't from around here. He had only arrived months ago from upstate. Hearing this, Malcolm had offered him the job.

Returning to the reception desk with a cup of coffee, Daryl found a man wearing a blue security guard uniform chatting to the nurse he had spoken to earlier. The man turned and seemed to recognize Daryl, offering his hand in greeting as Daryl approached.

"Daryl!" the man said, giving him a firm handshake. "I'm Reggie. I work the evening shift on this floor and have for years. Malcolm said that you a country boy from upstate."

Perturbed by the question, Daryl replied, "No, I'm just from upstate, not the countryside."

Slapping Daryl's shoulder, Reggie said, "Well, if it ain't here, it might as well be the country." Reggie gave a hearty laugh, amused by his own joke. "C'mon, I'll show you the lockers downstairs and get you your new uniform."

Reggie and Daryl took the elevator to the basement level and then made their way down a narrow hall to the locker rooms used by the hospital's staff. Daryl could hear the building's furnace working in a room not far from the lockers.

"Oh, that. That's the old furnace room," Reggie said, noticing Daryl's distractedness. "The morgue is down here too. The orderlies bring the bodies to the morgue and medical waste is disposed of in the furnace. I don't like to stay down here for too long. The air ain't right."

Reggie handed Daryl a hospital guard uniform from an empty locker and then told him that the locker was his. He then gave him a set of keys and a heavy flashlight, saying that he might need to enter a locked room during the night or that there could be a sudden power outage.

"The lights on that floor ain't so good. Once you change, we'll go upstairs and I'll give you the tour. While you do that, I need to use the commode." Reggie then disappeared around a corner.

Daryl changed out of his street clothes and folded them, placing his shirt and pants at the bottom of the locker. The guard uniform was snug but fit well enough. *I just need to lose a few pounds*, Daryl thought as he crouched to tie his shoes.

The two men walked back to the elevator and Reggie pushed the button for the top floor. They waited in silence as the elevator descended.

"Reggie? What are those symbols on the building, out in front?" Daryl said, almost unconsciously. "I saw a plaque to the hospital's founder. At least that's what I think it was."

"That? Well, that's the dedication to Nathaniel Wingate. He was an eccentric old railroad tycoon from the turn of the century. He paid for the building, but only if it was built on this here spot, facing the bay. Like I said, he was eccentric." Reggie chuckled as if remembering a joke.

"But what are those symbols carved into the stone? Are they religious symbols?"

"I don't know. Never noticed 'em," Reggie said, shrugging. "But there are some crazy rumors I've heard over the years

28

about old Wingate. One is that he was buried under the hospital basement at his own request."

The door to the elevator opened, taking Daryl and Reggie upstairs again. Reggie showed Daryl the wings on the thirteenth floor, pointing out which ones held critical or terminal patients.

"And this here's the cancer ward. You might hear 'em cry out at night—they have mood swings, they vomit. I almost feel sorry for 'em," Reggie said, sighing. "But I ain't worked the late-night shift in years, ever since I got promoted."

The reception desk was vacant by the time Reggie and Daryl returned. "Well, that's it, my man. You're on your own. A nurse comes up here from the twelfth floor to check on patients, but the guard is the only staff member on duty most of the time. We've had budget cuts every year for the past few years, so you're it."

As the elevator door closed on Reggie, Daryl turned about, surveying the three hallways connected to the reception area on the now quiet floor. The ceiling lights flickered. Daryl decided to take a short break in the lounge room.

The coffee in the pot was starting to look stale, but Daryl didn't want to make more. He poured a cup for himself, smacking his lips at the bland taste after taking a sip. A battered TV set was sitting on one of the tables, so Daryl walked over to turn it on.

The television set crackled, projecting a black and white static image. Daryl turned its knobs and adjusted the antenna, but no picture or sound would come in. *Must be bad reception on this floor. Maybe it's because we're so high up*, Daryl considered.

A long groan echoed from outside the lounge as Daryl took another sip of coffee. He cautiously stood up from his chair, emptied his coffee cup, and opened the lounge door to see where the groaning was coming from.

The sound had grown louder, emanating from one of the rooms in the cancer ward. "My God, oh God, save me," an old man pleaded, moaning pitifully between cries. "Please, make it stop, my God."

Daryl stood in the hallway and listened. *He'll wake up the other patients, but they're probably used to it by now. I don't know what else I can do. Maybe he'll stop soon.*

The ceiling lights flickered as Daryl turned a corner. At the other end of the otherwise empty hallway was a diminutive old woman wearing a hospital gown. Her hair was matted and she was barefoot, as if she had just gotten out of bed.

Daryl was about to call out to the woman when the lights flickered again, placing the hallway into darkness for a moment. When the light returned, the woman was halfway down the hall. Daryl could now see that the old woman's face was white, her eyes dull and staring. Her mouth hung open in a sloppy gape.

Horrified, Daryl turned and sped around the corner. The ceiling lights flickered once more, throwing the hallway before him into pitch black. When the lights burst suddenly back to life, the old woman stood directly in front of Daryl's, her face inches from his. She opened her cancerous mouth wide as if to scream, letting out a hideous, raspy gasp instead.

Stumbling, Daryl fell back toward the wall behind him, waving his arms in terror. The old woman stepped forward just as the lights flickered. All at once, she was gone.

Daryl leaned against the wall, breathing hard, looking around in a panic. *What the hell was that?* he asked himself once he could form a coherent thought. *Am I seeing things already?*

Checking both hallways, Daryl steadied himself and made his way back to reception. The elevator chimed and opened just as he arrived, a nurse wearing a white uniform and cap stepping out.

"Good evening, I'm Nurse Gabrielle," the young woman said, her words soft and smoothly accented. "I'm here to check on the ward patients." She looked Daryl up and down as he stood by the reception counter, a clipboard held at her side. "You're new on this floor, aren't you?" she queried. "Are you all right?"

"Um, why, yes, I'm fine. Just adjusting to the late-night shift. Too much coffee makes me jittery. Please, make your rounds and do whatever else you need to do. And my name's Daryl." Daryl then offered her a weak smile, doing his best to stop shaking.

"Pleased to meet you, Mister Daryl. And thank you, I appreciate that. I'll come back around once I'm done. See you in thirty." The young nurse sashayed away, flashing Daryl a quick smile as she turned the corner and disappeared.

Daryl listened to her footsteps echoing past the lounge room and fading as she reached the cancer and hospice wards. He decided to make a fresh pot of coffee and offer a cup to Miss Gabrielle.

Searching the lounge cabinets, Daryl found a jar of coffee, noting the smiling man with a freshly brewed cup on the label. The coffee maker percolated, and Daryl reached for a clean mug at the back of the cabinet.

Pouring hot coffee into a disposable cup, Daryl turned from the counter as the ceiling lights flickered. Corpses filled the room: some slumped into wheelchairs, others covered by translucent plastic sheets. Their mouths and eyes creaked open, an awful dead-gray pallor spreading over their expired flesh.

The coffee cup fell from Daryl's hand as the room went dark. The lounge was empty when the lights returned a moment later. The sound of approaching footsteps broke Daryl from his terrified, semi-catatonic state.

"You spilled your coffee, Mister Daryl. Mister Daryl?" Nurse Gabrielle stood in the doorway to the lounge, waiting for Daryl to notice her.

Daryl stared in a daze at the muddy pool of coffee on the floor and then turned. "I . . . I'm just feeling light-headed. I'm not used to being up this late at night." Daryl could only imagine that what he had just seen was a waking nightmare.

"I hope you feel better, Mister Daryl. There is such a thing as too much coffee. If it's all right with you, I'll leave you to your duties." Nurse Gabrielle closed the lounge door, the echo of her footsteps following her.

The elevator chimed as Daryl walked down the hallway, trying to shake the vision of the gray bodies. *There's a chance she'll tell Malcolm about this. I have to get my head together.*

Daryl stood at the reception counter, alone once more. He moved back and forth, scanning the hallways, telling himself he just needed to get used to being alone this late at night. He was seeing things, but that didn't mean any of it was real.

The elevator chimed again and Daryl turned. *She's back so soon? Maybe she forgot her clipboard,* Daryl thought, mildly pleased at the prospect of seeing Nurse Gabrielle again. A feeling of relief came over him for a moment.

The doors parted, revealing an empty wheelchair. Daryl felt the hairs on the back of his neck bristle as a profound terror seized him. Impulsively, without a thought, Daryl walked to the elevator and stepped inside.

The doors closed, and the elevator descended to the hospital's basement. When the doors opened, Daryl stared into a dark hallway, the distant sound of the hospital's overworked furnace heaving and bellowing somewhere in the dark.

The elevator doors closed behind Daryl and the elevator began its quiet ascent. From the shadows of the dimly lit hallway, tortured figures began to emerge.

Many were nude while others were garbed in hospital gowns. For some, the means of their deaths were clear; for others, it wasn't certain. As Daryl stood motionless, the mob of corpses rushed forward without warning. Cold fingers closed around his arms and Daryl cried out as he was hoisted above their heads like a prized trophy.

Half-crazed, Daryl's voice died. As if in a dream, he watched the ceiling blur past as he was carried to the waiting furnace room. One of the corpses near the front of the throng began to speak in a deranged and inhuman voice, reciting a ritual prayer:

> *"We consecrate this sacrifice to our Most Beloved, our Benefactor. The One who will grant us Eternal Life, so that we may again walk among the Living. Accept this oblation, which will be burned as an offering to you, Most Unholy One, Most Unholy One!"*

Daryl was hurled into the open furnace by the hands of the multitude. As the fire consumed him, he could only shriek in agony.

The undead stood before the furnace as it spat licks of fire, the ashes of Daryl's charred flesh floating through the air before it. The corpse who had recited the litany closed the furnace door and the horde of apparitions shuffled away, melding into the basement's mournful shadows.

Malcolm stood at the punch clock outside his office in the early morning and punched Daryl out at the end of his shift. The hospital was still sparsely staffed at this time, and no security guard had punched in yet for the day shift.

Turning the handle of the restroom sink faucet, Malcolm let cold water run into his open palms and then splashed it onto his face. He looked into the mirror, wondering whether he would be able to fill Daryl's position without another long vacancy. As he dried his face with a paper towel, a talisman fell from beneath Malcolm's shirt. Its jade surface was covered with strange letters and symbols.

Forged in Fire

Preston Winscott folded his copy of *The Times*, having just read the front-page news. There had been another murder at the city docks, this one as gruesome as the last. For months, a vicious killer had terrorized the city, slaying apparently at random. The victims all occupied lower social strata but otherwise had nothing in common. All had been found with missing organs and all had died with their throats ripped out. The police had no suspects and no leads, so the killer remained at large.

"You, young Winscott, have you read about the latest homicide down by the docks?" Gerald Hoskins approached Winscott as he sat in their club's drawing room on one of its palatial leather seats. Winscott had recently been inducted into the gentlemen's society of which they were both members. "This time, it was a street hawker," Hoskins continued, in his characteristic gruff manner. "The poor boy was found lying among his newspapers and wares. A bloody mess, like the others."

"Yes, Mr. Hoskins, I'm afraid I have," Winscott replied as he looked up at the older man. "This is the fourth victim now, isn't it?" Hoskins was a club officer and a close confidant of its founder, John Fallada. *"The Times* has been following the case. It's all been very sensational."

"I hope they catch him soon. Whomever it is is a madman and deserves to hang," Hoskins said pointedly. He then walked away, seating himself among several other society members engaged in riotous conversation, their copies of *The Times* in hand or nearby.

Winscott had joined the Argentum Club to socialize with others who shared his interest in natural science and the arts. A newly graduated medical doctor, Winscott was a man of relatively modest means but had nonetheless been inducted by the members with unanimous support. Owing to his quick mind and encyclopedic knowledge of the biological sciences, Winscott had won entry into the society where many others of his age and social standing had been turned away.

Taking out his pocket watch, Winscott checked the time: he needed to be back at the surgery in one hour. Winscott left the club and walked several blocks to a horse-drawn tram. He rode it back to the city hospital where he was employed. His mentor at the hospital, Doctor Arthur Burton, was waiting there for him.

"Doctor Winscott, so good of you to join us. You're late." Doctor Burton stood with the trainees in the surgery, their patient under anesthesia lying between them on the table. "You'll only need observe; this is a procedure you haven't yet needed to attempt outside of your studies."

The room reeked of bodily fluids. *The man on the table must have an infected limb*, Winscott decided. The patient was aged and bare under the white cloth that covered his midsection. Winscott placed a handkerchief over his nose and watched as a trainee doctor opened a leg wound, yellowish-white pus oozing forth from it. A second trainee doctor gagged, his mouth covered by a hanky.

After their session, Doctor Burton asked Winscott to meet him in his offices adjoining the surgical room. "Next time, you'll have to perform the same procedure by yourself while under my observation," Doctor Burton told him.

"The medical profession has made great progress these last few decades, I'm happy to say," Doctor Burton enthused. "That man would have likely lost his limb under unspeakable agony if we hadn't been able to sedate him and treat the inflammation." Doctor Burton slipped a vest and suit coat over his clean linen shirt before sitting.

"Medical school opened my eyes to these advances, Doctor Burton. I can only imagine what this new century may bring," Winscott said warmly, having already seated himself before Doctor Burton's desk.

Doctor Burton seemed concerned, as if his mind carried a heavy weight. "Winscott, you're aware of these terrible murders taking place around the city docks, are you not? The victims have all been found mutilated." Doctor Burton paused, peering into Winscott's face as if waiting for his reply.

"Why, yes, of course, Doctor Burton. The entire city is on edge over the homicides. I've been reading *The Times* for daily updates." Winscott thought it odd that Doctor Burton would even ask; everyone had heard of these murders. They were without precedent in the city's recent history.

"You're right. I only wanted to put into context what I'm about to tell you," Doctor Burton said, a hint of trepidation entering his voice. "I've been in contact with the commissioner at Scotland Yard and the detectives assigned to the case. Certain details have been made available to the newspapers, while others haven't. As head surgeon here, I've helped perform the autopsies on the deceased victims in each instance." Doctor Burton was now noticeably uncomfortable—a slight sheen of sweat glimmered on his forehead, and he kneaded his fingers into his palms.

Winscott frowned, afraid of where the conversation was going. "The articles have mentioned organs extracted from those killed, which is bizarre in and of itself," Winscott remarked, "but what else could have been left out if the police were willing to divulge such a morbid particular?"

"The police could only hide so much about the conditions of the bodies as the victims' remains were found by members of the public. However, the autopsies I completed on the dead have revealed a horrifying detail: the missing organs were likely eaten—directly from the wounds of the deceased." Doctor Burton's previously worried expression became one of visceral disgust.

"Why, that's horrible," Winscott blurted out. "So, the police are dealing with not only a killer but a cannibal as well?"

"Yes, it appears so. The detectives considered consulting an alienist, but for now they want to know if we have ever found any bodies that had been defiled like this. The remains dredged up from around the docks area often end up here," Doctor Burton explained, relieved to finally tell another the terrible secret he had been holding close to his chest.

"So, if I may ask, why are you telling me this, Doctor Burton? I would surmise that this is information the police would want to keep hidden from the public. As head of surgery, you should be able to let the police know what they need to help solve the murders." Winscott didn't want to seem insubordinate, but he was surprised Doctor Burton would relate any of this to him at all.

"Winscott, the police have reason to believe the murderer is possibly connected to the society you've recently joined, the Argentum Club," Doctor Burton revealed. "The only witness has been kept out of the papers in the hopes the killer will become overconfident and careless. The witness claims to have seen a man leave the docks near the scene of a killing before returning to your club. It was the most recent murder, from last week."

"Who is the witness that the police are protecting?" Winscott queried, now intrigued by all of this, even though his previous fear was not yet relinquished.

"No name was provided to me, of course, but the witness is another street hawker, a companion of the young boy who was slain," Doctor Burton confided. "He followed a man he described as 'dressed as a fine gentleman'—that is, wearing a top hat and cape. The man headed through the night streets to the back of the Argentum Club. The man slipped through a door behind the club, apparently.

"On this particular night, a heavy fog had set in, preventing the boy from seeing more than how the man was dressed," Doctor Burton continued. "The boy later reported his dead friend to the police. He had heard screaming, but by the time he arrived, there was only the suspicious gentleman leaving an alley nearby. As you can imagine, a gentleman would be quite out of place in that down-market part of town."

"So, what do the police want me to do? You've just described nearly every member of the club: 'a top hat and cape.' There must be a few hundred members now. The club has grown so much over the last twenty years." Winscott seemed rather proud as he relayed this fact.

"And I'm sure much of that is due to the prominence of your club's founder, Mr. Fallada," Doctor Burton said plainly. "That's the other issue: the police only have the word of a young boy, and an impoverished one at that. They can't search the club and question its members based on the unsubstantiated accusation of an urchin.

"Besides, Mr. Fallada is quite wealthy—he could possibly buy immunity for one of his members unless a compelling case is leveled against him. It's all just too much for the police to manage themselves, and this is their only lead, however tenuous. If you have any suspicions or observe anything, they want to know about it." Doctor Burton then gave Winscott a hint of a smile, hoping to gain his assent.

"Well, I'll do what I can. I'm still a junior member and I'm not privy to all that much. If I see or hear anything dodgy, I'll tell you right away." Winscott hoped Doctor Burton would be pleased with this answer and then just forget about the entire matter. The idea that one of the Argentum Club members, all accomplished men in their respective fields, was stalking the city docks, slaughtering the downtrodden, and then cannibalizing their remains seemed preposterous.

"By the way: *Fallada*. What kind of name is that? He's certainly not a member of the gentry. Is Mr. Fallada a foreigner?" Doctor Burton was polite when he said this but seemed more than simply curious.

"He has foreign roots, I'm told, but was born here," Winscott replied, casually repeating what he had heard from club members. "It seems he's descended from an Iberian princeling or something of the sort. His family made their fortune in precious metals generations back."

After attending to patients and completing his rounds, Winscott left the hospital later that evening. The fog was thick in the city streets, rolling past him as he walked to his residence nearby. *If the killer is a member of the Argentum Club, who might it be?* pondered Winscott, brushing the idea from his mind almost as soon as he thought of it.

The crowd was larger than Winscott had supposed it would be. Perhaps fifty or more people were facing the low stage: nearly a packed house. Winscott was skeptical about being here at all, let alone about the likelihood of learning anything worthwhile. His fellow member of the Argentum

Club, Foster, had invited him to this demonstration on mesmerism. Winscott regretted attending as soon as he sat down near the stage, his chair in the front row.

"There you are, Winscott." Foster stood in the room's threshold, dressed in his winter suit. "I'm so glad you could make it. I'm sure you won't be disappointed." All smiles, Foster took the empty seat next to Winscott and then scanned the room behind them. "Quite a turnout. The mesmerist should be here soon."

"Why did I let you invite me here, Foster? And why do you believe in this fashionable nonsense," Winscott lamented, asking the second question in a lower tone of voice. "Aren't you a naturalist? You should be pressing butterflies, not obsessing over this bunk."

A woman sitting behind Winscott whispered sharply to her male companion as if angered by the opinion Winscott had just expressed.

"Just have an open mind, Winscott. Once you witness a demonstration of mesmerism, you'll be completely convinced of its veracity." Foster then stood to greet someone sitting nearby. Several minutes passed before he returned, nearly levitating with anticipation.

Soon, a man arrived on stage, smartly dressed and carrying a compact leather briefcase. He placed the briefcase on the table at the stage's center. On either side of the table stood a plush velvet chair, much like those used by the audience.

The man opened the briefcase and took out several items he then placed on the table, too small to be seen clearly from where Winscott was seated. The man then turned to the assembly and raised his arms in welcome.

"Good evening, ladies and gentlemen. I'm so glad that you have come. My name is Alexander Beaumont. I was both a protégé and close confidant of the late Madame Obolensky, as well as a senior member of her Society of Harmony.

Her society for the inquiry into spiritual matters and life after death continues after her recent and most unfortunate demise.

"This evening, I will provide a demonstration of the enlightened science of mesmerism, of which both Madame Obolensky and I are—were, in her case—ardent devotees. The practical application of mesmerism can cure physical ailments, heal the broken mind, and reveal secrets of which even the subject may be unaware.

"All I ask for is a volunteer from the audience, chosen at random, who is willing to show everyone gathered here today the power of this technique and demonstrate what it can do for the healthy and afflicted alike."

A young woman in the audience stood up immediately, calling out, "Me, Mr. Beaumont. I volunteer." She then strode confidently toward the stage and stood next to Beaumont, waiting for permission to take the seat next to the table.

Beaumont seemed surprised, as if he hadn't anticipated such an eager response. "All right then, Miss. What's your name, if I may ask?"

The young lady replied enthusiastically, "Penelope Matthews, at your service."

The audience chortled in response, enamored at this fetching young girl's bravado.

"Pleased to make your acquittance, Miss Matthews. Now, please, remove your fine hat—place it on the table here—and sit very still in this chair." Beaumont then reached for one of the objects he had left on the table earlier.

Penelope seated herself and Beaumont took the other chair, facing her. He produced a coin pendant on a silver chain which dangled as he held it. "Relax and breathe out slowly, Miss Matthews. I'm going to mesmerize you with this charm. You will go to sleep, and when you wake, you will remember none of this. But when I tell you to wake up, you'll awaken instantly."

Staring fixedly at the oscillating pendant, Penelope became quickly and visibly heavy-lidded as the charm swayed rhythmically in Beaumont's grasp. She slowly entered a state of repose, and the audience hushed as they watched, spellbound.

Winscott whispered softly to Foster, "What's that necklace he's using? It looks ancient."

"I don't know," Foster murmured. "The coin on the chain might be from a museum."

"Now, Miss Matthews, you are asleep," said Beaumont in a calm, steady voice. "Please, tell me, are you asleep, Miss Matthews?"

Penelope answered Beaumont in a faraway voice, "Yes, I am asleep."

A low gasp rippled through the audience as they heard her reply.

"Good. Miss Matthews, we're going to go back into your past: to any place or time before this one. Allow your mind to wander and find a memory. Once you've found it, please tell me what it is and where you are." Beaumont still held the silvery pendant, but it was now hanging loosely from his hand.

Penelope's head began to turn back and forth as it rested against the back of the chair. Her lips began to move until, steadily, sounds emerged. "I'm somewhere in a dark forest. I'm chasing something, running very fast."

Beaumont remained calm. "Miss Matthews, please tell us more. Is there anyone with you? What are you chasing in those woods?"

"I'm not myself . . . I'm something else," Penelope replied, her voice sharpening, growing loud and shrill. "There are wolves around me. Large black wolves. It's night, and we're hunting."

There were audible gasps from the audience. Winscott looked around; many seemed visibly startled or upset.

Beaumont was taken aback, as if this was entirely unexpected. "Miss Matthews, are you sure that this is your memory and not just a bad dream? How do you know that this is you?"

Penelope's head turned back and forth as before. Abruptly, she stopped. Her eyes shot open. Her pupils were gone, her irises now completely white, as if she were blind. Penelope then growled in an animalistic voice, "Let me show you."

Leaping forward from her chair, Penelope grabbed Beaumont by his throat, sending them both tumbling to the stage floor in a clatter. Snarling savagely, Penelope clawed at Beaumont's eyes and bit at his face, the stunned Beaumont defenseless as he lay sprawled on his back.

Men from the audience rushed to Beaumont's aid while others ran screaming from the conference room. One woman fell to the floor in a faint. Three men had to pull Penelope from Beaumont, his face bloodied as she flailed wildly.

Beaumont climbed to his feet and cried, "Penelope, you will wake now!" Penelope abruptly went limp in the arms of the men who had restrained her. She slowly opened her eyes and, seeing the blood covering Beaumont's face, recoiled in disbelief.

Wiping his face with a cloth handkerchief, Beaumont winced and then asked the men to let go of Penelope.

"Are you sure, sir? This madwoman nearly killed you." The bearded man in a black suit held Penelope cautiously, a hand under one of her arms.

"Miss Matthews isn't at fault. The mesmerism session must've gone awry. Please, place her in the chair and let her go. She is her sweet young self again." Beaumont examined his face with his fingers, touching shallow slash wounds and wincing in pain once more.

The men carefully put Penelope back in her chair by the table and stood guard nearby. Penelope looked about the room before burying her face in her hands, sobbing uncontrollably.

Winscott and Foster had watched all of this unfold, too surprised to have intervened in time. Winscott saw the silver coin pendant lying on the floor near the stage, cast aside during the utter chaos that had unfolded mere moments before. The image on the silver coin was that of a she-wolf suckling her two cubs. Before anyone could see him, Winscott snatched up the pendant and quickly left the room.

"That was quite a ruckus at the Arts Club. One of their open conferences for discerning members of the public, I presume." Doctor Burton spoke to Winscott from behind his desk, having recently returned from the surgery. His mood seemed to have improved since their last encounter, when he had first told Winscott about the cannibal killer.

"That poor woman who went mad is in an asylum now, at least temporarily. And we both know what it's like in there." Winscott thought back to that evening, disquieted at the shocking scene he had witnessed.

"Well, Winscott, do you have anything for the police? I mean, do you have any suspects at the Argentum Club so far? Even anything uncertain you've seen?" Doctor Burton seemed hopeful.

"No, nothing," Winscott replied offhandedly. "I think the police may have been led astray by that street urchin. There hasn't been another murder by the docks since last month and I've found no reason to suspect anyone at the club." Winscott believed this answer would satisfy Doctor Burton, finally.

"You know, the police detective working on the case brought something quite interesting to my attention," Doctor Burton said carefully, his eyebrows rising as he spoke. "Every time there's been a murder by the docks, it's been on a night when the moon was full. The victims were found early that morning or during the day, but it seems the murders were done under the moon's full illumination. The newspapers haven't yet picked up on this pattern."

Winscott appeared puzzled. "When's the next full moon?"

Doctor Burton replied, "On Christmas Day. Will there be a gathering at your social club then?"

"Yes, but likely early in the evening," Winscott answered. "Married members will be at home with their families soon afterward. Since I'm still a bachelor, I'll probably remain longer. There will likely be a few revelers staying late, with nowhere else to go."

"Stay and see if you notice anyone leaving late," Doctor Burton requested, then becoming quiet for a moment as if unsure whether to ask some troubling question. Finally, he said, "Can you tell me more about Fallada?"

"Why do you ask? Do you suspect him?" Winscott again seemed puzzled.

"No, I don't suspect anyone," Doctor Burton reassured Winscott. "It's just that there's more to his background than most realize, including your club members. There are reasons to believe he's a naturalized citizen, not native-born, and that his family has rather unsavory connections—more than most might suspect. I have contacts in the Civil Service, and they did the necessary research for me."

"I've only met Mr. Fallada once," Winscott stated distantly, remembering the past encounter. "When I was first inducted into the society. He was a very well-spoken, charming man, quite supportive of my candidacy. But he's not really there all that much, it seems. Generally, it's Mr. Hoskins who keeps things running."

"Well, keep an eye on Mr. Hoskins as well," Doctor Burton urged. "We'll see if anything comes of Mr. Fallada soon. The police are going to stake out the docks on Christmas Day and station an officer outside of the Argentum Club. But the docks are such a large space, and they only have so many men.

"If you see Mr. Fallada or anyone else leave the club alone late that night, please follow him and see where he goes," Doctor Burton further enjoined, his voice becoming low. "The police can't spare any more men on what is only guesswork at the moment. They'll be working undercover, not in uniform."

Walking up the steps to the Argentum Club's front doors, Winscott noted the busy street beyond. Tonight, there would be a Christmas social, and Winscott would see John Fallada and many other members of the club in one place.

A magnificent Christmas tree stood in the drawing room's center, the room's rich furniture having been moved aside to make space for it. Winscott observed club members beginning to congregate. Many were served drinks from trays by demure waiters, and all spoke haltingly among themselves. Winscott reached into his suit breast pocket and touched the silver pendant, still unsure whether it was to blame for that young woman's transformation into a rabid beast.

Winscott continued surveying the drawing-room, pondering who the killer might be, assuming he was here at all. Most club members were entirely unassuming, so it did little good speculating on their criminal natures without evidence. These men possessed no peculiarities that might implicate them in the murders. As for those who did stand out, they hardly seemed the murderous sort. There were several, however, who did warrant consideration—and they were at the Christmas party tonight.

There was Mr. Stevenson, who had a very unpleasant personality and had often made unfavorable comments about "the lower classes." But violent enough to have committed these murders? Almost unbelievable.

Then there was Mr. Chapman, who was quite a suspicious character, making queer pronouncements and slinking about at gatherings. But he was more of an eccentric and not someone who could be considered dangerous. Just an oddball.

And then there was Mr. Hoskins. Short-tempered, coarse to the point of rudeness at times, and always keeping irregular hours. The last one to leave the club at night, almost without fail, but usually to his waiting carriage. It wasn't unimaginable that he could take a life but, again, the carnage around the docks was beyond what even a man like Mr. Hoskins was capable of. *There's probably no killer here at all,* decided Winscott.

Winscott then saw Mr. Fallada enter the room—it was only the second time he had seen him in person. Silver-haired and wearing a charcoal-gray suit, Fallada beamed as he strode in, greeting club members earnestly and then joining Mr. Hoskins near the bar cart. He leaned in to speak into

Mr. Hoskin's ear for a moment, then left to converse with someone else.

As the early evening hours passed, club members began to leave for their homes and private family celebrations. Mr. Fallada approached Winscott to welcome him. "Winscott, it's so good of you to make an appearance at our annual Christmas soirée. The new members often consider this event optional. I can assure you that it is not."

"I'm pleased to be here, Mr. Fallada. I wouldn't have missed the club's Christmas social for anything." Winscott tried to smile as Fallada shook his hand, but the older man's intensely steady gaze made Winscott uncomfortable. Shooting a quick glance away from Winscott's face and down toward his chest, Fallada then walked away without saying another word.

Foster had been watching the pair. He walked up from behind Winscott and said, "So, how are you, old boy?" and slapped him on the back. "I haven't seen you since the debacle at the Arts Club. I hope you don't blame me for what happened."

"No, not at all. No one could have seen that coming. I'm still just a bit worried about the girl, that's all." Winscott wanted to give Foster his attention, but he was still distracted by his unsettling exchange with Fallada only moments ago.

"Her parents should be able to extricate her from the asylum soon. As I understand it, the alienists want to ensure she's not a threat before releasing her." Foster gave a tight smile. "So! Any plans for later this evening?"

"I think I'm going to stay late here. Enjoy the holiday festivities and all that." Winscott was able to smile this time—he hoped that would be enough to make Foster leave him alone.

"There won't be too many left later tonight. Only old Hoskins and the other hangers-on. See you around the club again soon, what?" Foster turned his back and then made his way toward the open doors leading to the foyer.

The hours passed, and club members continued to leave, with Winscott finally standing near the Christmas tree by himself. Mummers could be heard out in the street going from door to door, bringing seasonal cheer:

We wish you a merry Christmas,

And a happy New Year,

A pantry full of good roast beef,

And barrels full of beer.

As the mummers' caroling faded away, Winscott noticed Hoskins pass through a curtain that led up a small flight of stairs to the club officers' personal chambers. Rank-and-file society members were only allowed on the club's second floor for induction ceremonies and other official matters.

What could Hoskins be doing? Winscott wondered as he watched his acquaintance pull the crimson red curtain aside, briefly revealing the steps leading up, and then vanish. *I've only ever seen him leave the club through the front doors and then take his carriage. And nothing's going on upstairs this late, that's for sure.*

Thinking quickly, Winscott decided to take a chance. He looked around and, confident the coast was clear, casually strolled toward the red curtain. With a final glance over his shoulder, he parted it and slipped inside. The sound of Hoskins' footsteps echoed from the floor above, and Winscott heard a door close.

The upstairs club room was empty, with the doors to the small private chambers along its hallway shut. *The door sounded like it was closed back here*, Winscott considered. He walked down a cramped staircase leading to a narrow back door. It was locked, and Winscott slid the bar loose before quietly cracking the door open and slipping his head out.

Soup-like fog rolled over the cobblestone street connected to the alleyway. The light from the full-risen moon remained mostly obscured by clouds drifting overhead, but nonetheless Winscott spied the silhouette of Hoskins walking slowly into the night, alone. Stepping into the alley, Winscott shut the door behind him and began following Hoskins at a distance.

Winscott skirted the glow of gaslight streetlamps, keeping to the shadows. Eventually, Hoskins entered an alley close to the docks district. Winscott stopped across the street, sheltered by an unlit shop's threshold. He hoped Hoskins would come out soon.

Instead, a guttural growl pierced the night, followed by a hideous cry and, finally, the sound of flesh being rended. Winscott remained tightly hidden as the screaming continued, panicked that he had found the real killer.

The screaming stopped and from the alley emerged a man dressed in a top hat and cape. He paused for a moment, looking both ways down the empty street. The man then slipped out of view, disappearing into the thick fog which billowed around him.

Hesitating, Winscott wondered if he should check the alley Hoskins had entered, almost sure of what he would find. *A dead end*, he thought, gulping, *no other way out*. He cautiously walked across the now silent street and peered into the gloomy alleyway, seeing what looked like mangled human remains among the dustbins and debris.

Hoskins, why him? Why was he out here all by himself? Winscott gasped as he began to retrace his steps, lost otherwise, following street signs and city landmarks back to the Argentum Club. He found the backdoor unlocked and stepped inside, standing in the dark space at the bottom of the stairs.

A light shone from the floor above. The stairway creaked as Winscott ascended, feeling both curious and afraid. It was past midnight; who could be at the club this late?

One of the chamber doors was cracked open, the room's light pouring out into the hallway. Winscott quietly moved toward the door, pausing a few paces from the entrance.

He heard a voice, Fallada's: "Please come in, young Winscott. I know that you're there."

Winscott froze in place, his legs made of stone.

"Don't just stand there in the hallway. Please do come in."

The door creaked open wider, as if moved by unseen hands. Winscott peeked inside and saw Fallada slipping on his suit coat, grinning. "Yes, come in. I've been waiting for you."

Winscott stepped inside. Fallada stood in front of him at his desk, wearing the same gray suit as earlier in the evening.

"I know you have the amulet. Please give it to me," Fallada requested, still grinning, the upright palm of his hand now outstretched.

"What happened to Hoskins? Was that you in the alley tonight?" Winscott sputtered in response, overwhelmed by what was happening to him.

"Hoskins had to be removed, I'm afraid. He knew too much about what happened with Madame Obolensky. Even after her death, she still has many devoted followers, and they were beginning to grow suspicious." Fallada let his hand fall to his side.

"Madame Obolensky? Were you responsible for her death?" Fear was starting to overcome Winscott, but he remained steadfast. He thought his life might depend on it.

"Yes. But 'Madame Obolensky' was actually a pseudonym. Her accent, as well as her entire persona, were affected. The woman was a charlatan and a quite well-paid one. But she *did* have this in her possession before I took it from her." Fallada reached into his breast pocket and produced a silver pendant, identical to the one recovered by Winscott at the mesmerism session.

"The old fraud had no idea what she really had at her bosom. But I did. Using this sacred artifact to perform mere parlor tricks . . ." Fallada shook his head, his face showing obvious disgust.

"You're the killer, Fallada," Winscott said firmly, angered that he could have been led into this web of deceit. "The police—they will corner you and eventually bring you to justice. But your charm, what does it do for its owner? Why would you kill to get it from that mystic?"

"This charm, as you call it, was forged in fire by my ancestors many generations ago. Indestructible, except in the place where it was created. The pendant was then lost for centuries, but we made every effort to find it. When we recently learned the silver pendant was held by Madame Obolensky, I took the necessary action," Fallada said, his expression gloating.

"But what does it give its user, you ask? Power. And immortality. To be free, and to be powerful, and, of course, to live forever. I am and will be forever, a true apex predator," Fallada declared, his eyes wide with exhilaration. "Now, if you please, Winscott, your silver pendant. As I said, I know you have it." Fallada grinned and stretched out his hand once more.

"How can we both have the pendant?" Winscott asked, panting, backing away as he touched his suit breast pocket. "Or is mine a copy?"

"A forgery, yes. Created by Madame Obolensky's disciples. But apparently with properties of the original, as the Arts Club found out. Now, please . . ." Fallada took a step forward, no longer grinning.

Winscott turned as if to run, but Fallada's words held him rooted to the spot. "Oh, don't try to leave, young Winscott. The outside doors are all locked. I've seen to that. You won't be getting out of here—not alive, at least."

The silver pendant in Winscott's suit pocket glowed with an eerie blue light, the radiance visible even from beneath the fabric. Fallada donned his own silver pendant, a heavy sweat forming across his brow.

"No one will ever find you, Winscott," Fallada taunted, his voice now low and growling. "Not that there'll be much of you left." Fallada dropped to his hands and knees, his suit ripping at its seams as he fluidly transformed into an enormous silver-and-gray-furred wolf. The chamber door then shut on Winscott as if of its own volition, blocking his escape.

The slavering beast stalked toward Winscott from across the room. Instinctively, Winscott reached into his suit pocket and held out the pendant for protection, its unearthly light intensifying as he did.

A candescent, blue-hued fog began to seep under the closed door, engulfing the floor as the gray wolf drew closer. Fallada stopped in his—its—tracks and began to snarl, as if under attack from the spectral mists. Other wolves formed from within the fog, snapping and biting at the gray wolf. Ghostly howls echoed from the walls of the room as more wolves materialized in the vapor and besieged their beleaguered opponent.

Fallada was seized on all sides. The fog wolves pounced, clawed, bared their teeth, and finally brought down the monstrous gray wolf. The still, nude form of a man was left lying on the carpeted floor as the mists receded. Winscott leaned over Fallada's corpse, removing the silver pendant from around his neck.

"You're not far, *señor*. You are near the castle. It's only a few miles north from here." The farmer had stopped his mule-drawn cart when Winscott hailed him. Winscott folded his map, thanked the man, and continued his journey on foot up the dusty and pitted road. He was glad to have finally found a local who could understand him this far from the city.

The imposing castle rose on the horizon, its towers jutting against a clear, blue, cloud-strewn sky. Winscott touched his shirt pocket, feeling the outline of the two pendants that rested therein. Soon, the silver pendants would be returned to the earth from which they had first been shaped, no longer the creations of men or of gods.

Where the Bayou Ends

"**I**t's your fault we're out of gas," Patricia exclaimed, slamming a closed fist against the car's dashboard. "We should've stopped when you spotted that last gas station. Your so-called 'shortcut' has only gotten us stranded in the middle of nowhere." Patricia looked down at the back of Michael's head, her expression incensed, but he ignored her rant. Seemingly undisturbed, Michael continued sorting through the glovebox's contents.

"Here. I think we're close to here," Michael said finally, moving an index finger along a network of lines on the map he had unfolded. "Or maybe here. If we can find someone with gas to spare, we can make it back to the highway. Then we'll be at your departed mother's plantation home before midnight."

Patricia sighed, exasperated.

"There's a gas tank in the trunk. Let me get it." Michael offered, avoiding Patricia's angry gaze. He leaned over to open the driver-side door before stepping out onto the dirt road.

Michael hurried to their sports coupé's roomy trunk, taking the car keys out of his pocket with a jingle. He propped the trunk open and searched through its packed storage compartment, objects clanging. Patricia waited sullenly up front, wincing at each noise.

Opening the passenger-side door and stepping out, Patricia straddled the hood, the car's bright headlights shining into the swampy woods around them. They were stuck on a deserted road and no one was in sight. How did she ever let Michael convince her that taking this circuitous route would save time? She'd rather have been late for the reading of the family will or even have missed it entirely.

As Patricia leaned against the car's front grill, deeply inhaling the humid night air, she saw a light in the distance. The light moved slowly between the sagging cypress trees, their heavy branches drooping above the marshy ground.

The curious orb of light bobbed and weaved, growing larger and then diminishing even as it seemed to stay the same distance from the car. The light drifted upward and sideways, disappearing for an instant behind a tree trunk. Then, without warning, the ball of light zig-zagged rapidly and winked out, the space among the trees entirely dark once more.

Rubbing her eyes, Patricia blinked, then peered into the nighttime woodland: the ball of light was gone, as if it had never been there. *What was that?* Patricia asked herself, scanning the tree line off the road. *That wasn't a flashlight or anything. It was too high above the ground.* Behind her, the trunk slammed shut, and Patricia momentarily forgot about the strange light.

Michael strode up, holding a red metal gas can by its handle. "Got it," he said triumphantly. "It was buried under the spare and some junk. I need to clean that trunk when we get home. Now, let's see if we can find someone with extra gas." He looked ahead hopefully, searching the dark road in front of them, the full moon providing some limited light. "There should be houses along this road somewhere."

Patricia rolled her eyes and clenched her teeth, shaking her head. She felt like screaming. "Michael, you have no idea where we are. We could be hiking along this road all night. And it's late; we can't just knock on someone's door and demand gasoline in the middle of the night."

"Hey, let's not fight now," Michael scolded, keeping his voice calm and measured. "Trust me. We'll find someone who'll help us. If there's a light on in the house window, we can knock. People stay up late in these parts."

Glancing at his wristwatch, Michael opened the car door to shut off the headlights and lock the doors. He then began walking down the road, not turning to see if Patricia was following him.

Patricia reluctantly went after him, pushing herself away from her seat on the car hood with a groan. The empty gas can clanked noisily as Michael's leg occasionally struck it.

Patricia, don't marry this fool, Patricia told herself as she glanced behind them. The ball of light had re-appeared, hovering again near the tree line. The light seemed to be trailing them from behind the trees, but it slipped into darkness as Patricia stopped to watch it.

"Michael, wait," Patricia ordered, now beginning to become afraid. "Come back. There's something behind us."

"You mean, like the swamp?" Michael said, still walking, not bothering to turn around.

"There was a light moving among the trees over there," Patricia said, anxious. "It's gone now, but I saw it right before you got the gas can too. I think it's following us." Patricia peered into the woods on either side of the narrow road, searching for another sign of the bizarre phenomenon.

"Patty, it's nothing," Michael admonished. "Come on, we need to find some gas." Michael had stopped to look at Patricia but now turned to trudge back down the road again, the hollow sound of the gas can banging against his leg echoing behind him.

"No, really, Michael. I think something's following us. We could be in real danger." Patricia ran up to Michael's side, glancing furtively behind.

The road's surface was uneven and there was a clear night sky overhead, the bright stars and full moon leading the couple. Michael hoped they'd find a house soon; if not, he realized they'd have to walk the length of the road back to the car and spend the night there.

There was a silence between them for some time, and then Michael asked, "How much do you think your mother left you? Is there a chance she might've left you out of her will altogether?"

Patricia stared ahead as they walked, not answering right away. "She could have. Lucas was always her favorite. I was Dad's favorite, but Dad died first. Lucas may have gotten everything, to the tune of several million."

"I hope not," Michael retorted. "Your spoiled brat of a younger brother doesn't deserve a dime of your family's money. He's never even had a job."

"I know," Patricia replied wearily. "But what can I do? Mom's last will and testament are legally binding."

"You can contest it," Michael suggested, his tone encouraging. "Retain a good attorney. Lucas is too much of a spineless twerp to put up a serious fight. He might not even know how to hire a lawyer."

Patricia laughed, looking up into the night sky as she did. "You may be right," Patricia said, smiling for the first time that evening. "I never saw him read anything but comic books when we were kids. Plus, he's a dropout."

Further up the road, Patricia spied a light flicker on in the window of a distant dwelling. "There, Michael!" Patricia blurted, pointing into the woods. "There's a house with its lights on. Let's check it out."

Michael nodded without saying anything, hopeful but tired from lugging the gas can over miles of bad road.

Michael and Patricia stepped off the dirt road and into its grassy shoulder, walking through an open field before reaching a line of cypress trees. The house was mostly hidden within its own grove—Patricia suspected it'd be almost unnoticeable during the day.

More a single-story shack than a house, the place was made of flimsy wooden planks and rested on a raised platform of sorts. A short set of steps led to its front porch, on which two rocking chairs were stationed as if guarding the entrance. The light came from a grimy window next to the front door.

"You really want to go in there? After seeing this place up close, I'm not so sure," Patricia said uneasily, glancing over at Michael as he put his gas can down on the grass.

"Of course, why not?" Michael replied, seemingly unfazed by the shack's ramshackle exterior. "I'm sure whoever lives here is friendly. People are very hospitable in these parts." Michael blithely walked up the steps and knocked on the shack's rickety door twice, pausing between knocks.

There was no answer. "Why don't you try the doorknob?" asked Patricia. "It can't hurt. If they really are friendly, that is." Patricia stood back in the shack's yard, hoping Michael hadn't naively led them into a difficult situation.

Michael tried the door's handle and it turned clumsily, improperly fixed into its socket. The door creaked open, revealing a solitary room with a round table, chairs, and some moldy furniture scattered about its corners. What looked like the dining room space was fully lit by a lantern hanging above the wood table. It cast long shadows across the room.

"Shall we go in? The lights are on, but no one's home—or so it seems, anyway." Michael opened the door wider and gestured for Patricia to step inside the shack. "If the owners come home, we can just say we got lost and sought shelter for the night."

"What if they shoot us dead instead?" Patricia countered, amazed at how oblivious Michael could be. Patricia began to think that this was the final straw and that a break-up was in order once the two of them returned to civilization.

Michael walked in and looked around, ignoring Patricia's question. The walls of the shack were covered with mounted deer heads and other hunting trophies, wood carvings, and what appeared to be old family portraits in tarnished frames. An elaborate cuckoo clock, out of place in the shack's otherwise dingy interior, was fixed prominently on the opposite wall. Next to the clock was a second door facing them, behind the wood table and chairs.

"Look, there are some plates on the table," Michael said excitedly, gesturing toward a greasy pile of dishes and utensils. "It looks like someone's eaten dinner here, probably tonight. Maybe they'll be back soon?" Michael looked down at the pile of plates, surmising whomever it was had eaten here alone.

Patricia made a quick check of the front porch and the yard and then walked inside the shack to join Michael. "Shall we check the back room?" she proposed after surveying what was around her, her tone somewhat irritated. "If they're asleep and we wake them up, we'll get shot just the same as if we surprised them coming home."

Michael smirked, looked around the room for a second time, and then peeked out the front, not seeing anyone in the woods nearby. The sounds of croaking frogs and other, less visible wildlife filled the night, steady in the low din they made. "You first this time?" Michael requested, motioning toward the shack's back door.

Disregarding Michael's invitation, Patricia stepped out onto the front porch and examined the twin rocking chairs.

They were worn but in good repair, not neglected like the shack's outer walls and dilapidated roof. "We must be right near the mouth of the swamp's tributary in these woods," Patricia said aloud, her mind wandering for a moment as she spoke. "The cabin is likely built on a platform to keep it from sinking."

Without saying a word, Michael opened the back room's door, noting that Patricia was facing away from him on the porch. Michael then said in a quiet voice, almost whispering, "Patricia, come look at this." Patricia turned and saw Michael standing in the open doorway to the back room, staring down at something out of view.

Patricia joined Michael at the threshold of the room. Imprisoned in wooden cages on the otherwise bare floor were two children, a boy and a girl, perhaps ten years old. The children were filthy and dressed in ragged clothes but didn't appear to have been starved or otherwise maltreated. They leaned against the sides of their small cages made of tightly bound sticks, asleep.

"My God, what have we found?" Patricia gasped, at once searching for a way to free the children. Michael continued to stare down at the sleeping children, dumbfounded.

Rattling its bars, Patricia searched for a way to force the cage open in the unlit room. There was nothing else here except the two cages, a square window without curtains being the room's only other feature. There was also no door to either cage, nothing even for a young child the boy's size to crawl through to escape. How the children had even been placed inside the cages was uncertain.

As Patricia crouched, her hands on the cage bars, the boy abruptly opened his eyes, staring directly at her. He scrambled to his knees and, jabbing his fingers out between the fastened sticks, began screaming at Patricia.

"Let us out! Please, ma'am, we're trapped in here by our pa!" The boy was quite agitated, shaking his cage violently and clenching his teeth as he struggled to free himself. The girl woke and then began wailing, also grasping the stick bars.

Michael spoke for the first time since inviting Patricia into the room. "Let's get out of here, Patty. We can sleep in the car tonight. We'll be safe in the morning." Michael then began to back away, staring fixedly at the two now manic children as he crossed the door's threshold.

"No, Michael, we can't just leave them! These kids need our help. Someone's keeping them as prisoners!" Patricia kept feeling around the cage as the boy screeched, begging to be let out. She still couldn't find a latch or any obvious way to pry the cage open.

Finally, Patricia asked the boy, "You said your pa is keeping you trapped in here. Why did he put you in these cages? And where is your pa now?"

The boy was spitting as he cried and shrieked, mucus running from his nose. He then became calm enough to answer Patricia. "'Cause he's a scared a' us," the boy said, trembling. "Me and my sister, Violet. He says he needs to hold us in here after our mama died." Violet had also become quiet, as if waiting to see what might happen.

Stepping back into the room, Michael reached down to grab Patricia's shoulder. "C'mon, let's go," he said adamantly. "We can't get involved in this." Michael then tried to pull Patricia to her feet, but she resisted.

Firmly brushing away his hand, Patricia turned and stood up, facing Michael. "Michael, these children might die without us." She crouched again to search for an opening in Violet's cage. Both then heard a whistling sound coming from outside the shack, as if someone were humming a tune.

"Their pa, he's coming!" Michael said sharply, moving away from Patricia. "Close the door. We have to leave."

Patricia looked at the children with an apologetic expression and left to join Michael. The children cried as the door was closed on them but then hushed themselves, afraid of their pa.

Michael and Patricia began to rush toward the shack's door when they came face to face with an old man walking in from the porch. He carried a satchel over his shoulder and a battered shotgun slung over an arm. The old man recoiled in surprise when he saw his uninvited guests but then quickly leveled his weapon at them.

"Who are you folks?" the old man demanded, a finger on his shotgun's trigger. "How'd you get in?" The old man then wheezed and coughed, seemingly as frightened as he was angry at the intrusion.

"The door was open, sir," Michael replied quickly, carefully watching the shotgun barrel aimed at his chest. "Our car broke down. We saw the light and came in. We need help."

Michael and Patricia slowly put their hands up as the old man continued pointing his gun.

"It was, now, was it? 'Cause I always lock this here door when I leave. Otherwise, the possums get in." The old man backed up and reached to close the front door without looking behind him. He then steadied his shotgun in a two-handed grip, saying, "Both of you, sit down at the table. And no funny business neither."

Seeing no other choice available, Michael and Patricia took their seats on the tottering chairs, which were barely sturdy enough to support their weight. The old man stood not far from them, his shotgun at the ready.

"What're your names? You two married?" the old man questioned, studying Michael and Patricia with a cautious eye. He stepped closer to get a better look.

"Ah, no, we're engaged," Michael replied. "We were driving on the road to her family's home when we ran out of gas. If you have any to spare, we can just be on our way. My gas can is out in the yard and I have some cash to pay." Both Michael and Patricia nervously kept their hands visible on the table.

"You didn't take nothin', did you? You open that door?" The man waved his shotgun barrel toward the closed door which hid the two caged children.

"No, sir," Patricia replied, fighting to keep her face calm. "We had just walked in when we heard you whistling. Please, we don't want trouble. If you don't have any gasoline, we'll leave." Patricia tried to smile hopefully at the old man but managed only to look fearful.

The old man was silent as he continued to scrutinize Michael and Patricia. He suddenly turned to rack his shotgun on a wall mount and then took a seat at the table, putting his satchel down next to his chair. "Name's Eli. What's yours?" the old man said. Patricia noted that he didn't extend his hand.

"I'm Michael. And this is Patricia, my fiancé," Michael answered shakily, feeling relieved that their tense situation seemed to have defused. "Patricia's family is from farther down state."

"You don't say," Eli said keenly, his eyes now resting only on Patricia. "Then you've heard about these here woods? What happened here long ago?" Grinning, Eli revealed a patchwork of missing teeth.

Patricia glanced at Michael uncomfortably, wondering whether they had gotten out of a dangerous situation or not. "No, I don't," she said, "I mostly grew up away from my hometown and I've only come back for this trip. What happened here?"

"A terrible crime," Eli said, a touch of macabre sadness in his tone. "Two youngins, a boy and a girl, were done killed in cold blood by their pa. He then killed his wife too. The bodies, they were never found." Eli then sat in

66

silence, deliberately regarding Michael and Patricia before continuing with his tale.

"Their pa took his two youngins out into the bayou woods, where the bald cypress trees stand alone," he recited almost poetically, his voice growing more sinister. "He found a deep part near the shore, where the bayou ends, where the waters are dark and murky. He drowned the boy first and then his precious little daughter, without a drop of pity. Their small bodies sank, dragged down into the heart of the swamp itself.

"Next, he came back for his wife," Eli said as he went on, his words now hauntingly quiet, approaching a whisper. "She knew what he had done, so she stabbed him with a knife, cutting the man."

At once, Patricia noticed the faint scar impressed across Eli's nose and over his cheek; it looked like it had healed long ago.

"They fought for that blade and then the man stabbed his wife until she lay dead on the cabin floor," Eli pronounced, his voice trailing off. "He pushed her body out into the bayou waters, where it sank like a stone, lost forever . . . forever." Eli stared at a bare spot on the shack's floor, where the wood planks had been splintered as if hacked.

Patricia glanced at the wall behind Eli and saw a faded portrait hanging there, a grainy family photo. There was a man, his wife, and two children, a boy and a girl. The man was almost certainly Eli, but many years younger.

"Michael, run!" Patricia cried, leaping from her seat and dashing toward the closed door of the shack. She grabbed the spindly door's awkward knob and flung it open, running out into the swamplands, narrowly avoiding tripping over Michael's gas can as she went.

As Patricia ran, she heard no sounds of pursuit behind her, only the croaking of the bullfrogs and the peculiar calls of nocturnal birds. Under the moonlight, Patricia realized she couldn't find the road where she and Michael had first discovered the shack. It was gone.

The swamp's canopy hung over her as she thrashed at the dense woods surrounding the shack. The moonlight was bright above the trees, but she could no longer see the light from the shack, the close darkness of the woods enveloping her. Ahead was the bayou, languidly flowingly through the low woodland.

Patricia leaned against a cypress, the tree's fanning leaves rustling in the warm nighttime breeze. *No one is following me*, she thought. *Michael! He must have run out after I made it away*.

The moon's visible light grew dimmer as Patricia advanced further into the swampy woods, feeling the moist soil beneath her shoes sag, her footing unsteady. She again clung to a cypress tree to breathe easily, resting as her journey through the swamp's treacherous underbrush grew increasingly arduous.

There was a light ahead. It was quite small, almost a pinpoint, but Patricia could see it through the foliage swaying in front of her. The light was stationary. *Perhaps a handheld lamp or flashlight*, Patricia considered, worrying that whomever she might find could be a threat.

Struggling forward, Patricia climbed over moss-covered cypress roots and wild brambles, her feet beginning to sink. *It's soggy here, like muck. Got to watch where I step*, Patricia said to herself, now treading cautiously.

The clear moonlight sparkled over the bayou's waters, the pinpoint of light still ahead, unwavering. *There should be a shallow part here. But I'll still get wet*, Patricia decided, searching for a place to circumvent the bayou's waters.

The muddy waters seeped into Patricia's shoes, soaking her socks and feet. She was not quite waist-deep in the bayou's water when she began to reach the shore on the other side of the tributary, panicking briefly as something brushed against her leg in the fouled river.

Patricia could now see there were not one but two small lights beaming out from the dark. As she waded through the bayou's lily pad-covered surface, growing closer to the shore, the outline of a figure began to form. It was a young boy. He stood completely still by the water's edge.

Hurrying, the water splashing around her, Patricia paused her labored strides and peered at the shadowy figure. It was the boy from the shack, his thick hair now combed down over to one side of his face. The two lights came from the boy's eyes—they shone eerily in the darkness of the woods.

How did he escape from his cage? Patricia thought, startled. *And how did he get so far ahead of me?*

"Hello, it's me from the cabin," Patricia called out to the boy. "I'm almost to the shore. Can you grab my hand and help pull me in? I seem to be sinking."

The boy was silent. Too distraught to consider what might be happening, Patricia pushed forward but began to sink even further into the silt bed of the bayou. Standing waist-deep in the waters and within reach of the shore, Patricia now found she couldn't move.

This spot, it's like molasses. I'm being sucked under! Patricia realized, trying to press ahead but failing. The boy only continued to stand in silence, his eyes glowing with a whitish light as Patricia slowly sank below the bayou's surface.

"Oh, God! Save me! Don't just stand th—" Patricia's cries were cut off as her head slipped under the water with a gurgle, her body dragged beneath by the deadly trap. As she was submerged in the waters of the swamp, the boy watching over her untimely death vanished, the ripples on the surface now the only trace remaining of Patricia.

Eli opened the door to the shack and quickly glanced over the front yard littered with debris. The bullfrogs and other nighttime inhabitants of the woodland swamp croaked, hummed, and chirped, forming a discordant yet soothing chorus as Eli spied what he was looking for. He picked up the red gas can, returned to the porch, and placed the empty can next to his rocking chair.

Sliding into the chair's scooped seat, Eli gripped its armrests and began to rock back and forth. He went steadily, with no urgency—after a time, he reached into his overalls' bib pocket and removed a leather wallet and key chain. Examining Michael's driver's license, he decided he'd just burn all of it once he pushed their car into the swamp some miles down the road.

A whitish light soon bobbed near the tree line, swirling and then bouncing until it was joined by a second ball of palish light, weaving, circling, and finally hovering in place. Eli made a thin smile and stood up to go back inside the shack, whistling in anticipation.

There was a quiet knock at the door. Eli answered and found two young children, a boy and a girl, standing on the porch, gazing up at him. They smiled brightly, with the boy exclaiming, "Pa! We can come home now!" Eli smiled in return and then let his children inside, closing the shack's door after them.

Further Back and Faster

Holo-journal log number X67-L87

Our ship has landed. The journey took thirty-seven days due to our vessel's upgraded propulsion systems. I was chosen as this mission's navigator mostly due to my mathematical background rather than my practical experience; this is, after all, only the third mission I've ever flown on. I assisted the pilots by calculating the exact coordinates to descend onto this side of the planet's northern hemisphere.

The planet is as dusty and as barren as the imaginal catalog indicated: many shades of orange, red, and brown, with no water or vegetation in sight. Life may have existed here once, but it has long since disappeared. Our employer's interest is mainly in potential resource extraction, including new and previously unknown resources deposited beneath the planet's crust. Extracting these resources efficiently with the tools available may prove quite challenging.

With this mission, my life has made such a strange turn. That I would be here, off-world, in a geodesic dome surrounded by an expansive emptiness, ready to face such a daunting challenge. Now, as a young man, I've only just come into my own, no longer under the yoke of my overbearing father. He insisted I follow in his footsteps as an academic, but such a sedentary pursuit was not for me.

So, instead, I enrolled in the company's training program for interplanetary exploration and was one of the few selected for the mission. I've taken the ultimate risk by coming here, but with equally ample rewards. A real, thriving colony, not just a dome station, may one day be possible on this planet. Such an achievement depends on our further research and what is uncovered during our stay on this largely unexplored, stark wasteland.

Holo-journal log number X67-L88

It's 70 degrees Fahrenheit outside our dome now, which is practically a heat wave. The skeleton crew that ran Exploratory Station 3 before our arrival—Dalton, Rogers, and Russo—told us that the winters at the polar caps drop as low as minus 243 degrees Fahrenheit. Not that anyone could live on the planet's surface, even on the mildest summer day.

Since our arrival, Exploratory Station 3 has been humming with activity. Even though they were protected by their own magnetic fields, the previous company stations have been shut down due to savage dust storms and, ultimately, obsolescence. We are alone here, the only life on a barren planet so far away from home.

No national governments maintain bases here; their available funds are now far outstripped by those of private interests and multinational corporations. So, this planet's long-term development is in the hands of free enterprise, what little remains of it under current global economic conditions.

Selected members of our crew of thirty will begin to make exploratory trips to the other hemisphere within ten sols, as scheduled. The skeleton crew warned us that past team members have been lost under difficult conditions in this hemisphere—three, in fact. We were briefed on these losses earlier by the company as a matter of legal indemnification and transparency.

The exoplanetary geologists hope to begin drilling within forty sols. Our mission is a year-long commitment, but we still need to make the best of our time. We can't come back empty-handed, or we will surely face consequences, likely severe. The scarcity of critical, non-renewable resources at home makes our mandate all the more urgent.

Holo-journal log number X67-L88.3

I had a very odd conversation with one of the geologists, Myers, this morning. He said he believed there was life here and that we just hadn't found it yet. And not just microbial life, but complex life, even sentient life.

I asked him where such life might be hidden, and he said, "Below the planet's surface." It's a disconcerting thought, but no one can rule out the possibility. What such life forms might be like, neither he nor I can say with any certainty. "Damn it, Jim. I'm an exogeologist, not an astrobiologist!" Ha.

This planet may have once been awash with life, its surface covered by churning oceans. It's older than our own, and life may have developed sooner and more rapidly here. The divergent chemical makeup of the planet would have no doubt made these life forms unlike any on Earth.

There's also the possibility that the planet's surface was once covered in colossal glaciers, which formed the impressions we've so far interpreted as now desiccated riverbeds. The entire planet could have been frozen solid for eons, inhospitable to even a bacterium. How the surface could have eventually dried out and become the present-day desert that it is also remains a mystery.

Holo-journal log number X67-L88.6

I just awoke from a dream. It's late in the night cycle, and most of the station's crew is asleep. I can't remember the details of it, but my dream was somehow related to the planned expedition into the southern hemisphere. Will the men be in danger there? I can't recall any of it now.

For years I kept a dream diary, something I never revealed to anyone, but an admission that is now being recorded in this journal. I've had many vivid dreams, some of which could more rightly be called nightmares. That I have this intuitive side to my mind is surprising, given my rational nature as a mathematician.

My father is a university professor, a geometer. His field of study is differential geometry, a branch of mathematics that studies the geometry of curves, surfaces, and manifolds. He would spend hours in this study, interrogating the nature of shapes, my long-suffering mother nearly forgotten.

Once, he told me that Euclidean geometry and other accepted mathematical explanations of the physical world were insufficient. That we had yet to discover the full breadth of material reality or even had only just scratched its surface. My father then confided mathematicians would someday derive a method of analyzing the complete vectors of space-time, so that faster-than-light travel and other modes of hyper-speed transport would become a possibility, at least in theory.

How could objects move so rapidly, unconstrained by the familiar laws of physics? And would such objects, moving at blinding speed, be visible to any potential observer? These questions may go unanswered.

Even in this age of off-world exploration, we are not much closer to a faster-than-light starship than in the century before us. My father said that such a device would need to "bend space," though he never gave more of an explanation than that. For the time being, all of this is merely conjecture.

But there is one dream I remember from years ago. I was afraid to write it down in my diary as I thought someone might find it. Some things are too unnerving to be set on paper, but I now sense what I envisioned should somehow be documented.

In my dream, the world was at peace, as it hadn't been in so long. Prosperity for the many was beginning to return. The catastrophic damage done to our natural environment over generations, slowly reversed. A new Golden Age, often hoped for in the past, might soon dawn on mankind.

As I walked, the sun was bright overhead. My mood was pleasant, and I recall feeling optimistic about the future. Then, the light dimmed, as if a total solar eclipse had occurred. The warmth drained out of my body where I stood, midday becoming nighttime.

Gargantuan ellipsoids filled the sky, flying lithic structures which might have been hewed from an unknown world's rocky core. As darkness fell, an intense, biting cold pervaded, frosting everything within sight. Soon, blistering, arctic winds came, battering glass buildings and burying city streets in a mantle of impenetrable snow.

People were frozen in place, resembling rimy wax figures of their real selves. In the near-total dark, penumbral shapes began to emerge, any other aspect of them hidden. The world had been cloaked in a perpetual night, as frigid as the deepest reaches of outer space.

And then I woke. I had dreamt a dream so lucid that it might portend an actual doomsday event. How could I see this? And why did the memory of this vision of worldwide destruction return to me now?

Holo-journal log number X67-L89.2

The exploratory team left this morning for the southern hemisphere, which is punctuated by many thousands of craters and inactive volcanoes. It's winter in the southern hemisphere, which will make a prolonged visit that much more demanding (as referenced in a previous log entry concerning the winter temperatures at the polar caps).

Fifteen members, including Captain Price, our pilot, and Dr. Brooks, the head of the scientific research team, comprise the exploratory team. The three rovers used for transport are highly durable, being able to withstand intense radiation and other hazards, including the southern hemisphere's dark winter. This region was quite active in the planet's early history and is the most likely place where vast mineral deposits lie untouched under the surface.

The rovers double as hovercraft and can make the trip in a single sol. This dusty planet is surprisingly small, which makes it even more surprising that its two hemispheres are so dissimilar from one another. The expedition should remain for approximately seven sols, returning after mapping two preselected regions more thoroughly for future excavation.

According to Dr. Brooks, there could be things in this hemisphere that may come as a complete surprise to the research team. The area has never been fully explored, either by the corporation's scientific staff or by earlier government-led expeditions; they're venturing into the unknown. They're brave men, indeed.

Holo-journal log number X67-L90

We've lost contact with the southern hemisphere exploratory team. The team signaled that they had arrived in the hemisphere, and we were able to chat with Captain Price over the rover's video feed, albeit with some interference. By the next sol, however, a massive, planet-wide dust storm coupled with electrical interference began to gather within our hemisphere and then started to spread over the globe. This was initially terrifying—we've all heard the skeleton crew's stories about these storms and what they can do.

Communication with the rovers has now become impossible, at least for the present. The team is trapped in the southern hemisphere during its winter solstice, when the night on this planet is longest. Before the comms failure, Captain Price indicated that the team had found unusual clefts and fissures in the area where they had arrived and intended to search them. I hope they are safe and that the team doesn't take any unnecessary risks with their lives.

JAMES DERMOND

Holo-journal log number X67-L96.8

Fourteen sols from last contact, we finally heard from
Captain Price and the exploratory team. The vast dust
storm had mostly dissipated, with electrical interference
low enough for remote communication to resume. Price
reported that they had lost a rover as well as its five
team members while sheltering from the dust storm. The
rover became trapped under the hemisphere's surface after
entering unmapped ice caverns, enormous and extending
for many miles. The team had discovered these caverns
while investigating the fissures mentioned in the last log
entry.

One fissure was large enough to be accessible by rover.
Entering, the crew found the fissure widened into a cave.
The rover's crew, which included Exogeologist Myers,
was designated to scout the cave. The team found that
it connected to a system of caverns below the planet,
something never discussed in documented research of the
southern hemisphere.

While underground, Myers' rover captured video images
of these primeval caverns, which tunneled deep into the
planet's crust. Price and his team, as well as Dr. Brooks' team,
were only able to receive the video images once they had
parked their rovers inside the fissure's cave, away from the
punishing dust storm and its atmospheric interference. It
seems the fury of the dust storm had uncovered the entrance
to the fissure, hitherto buried. We will have to search for
Myers' team again once it is safe to do so, but every man may
be lost for good.

Holo-journal log number X67-L97.5

The lead engineer, Jacobs, is examining the video footage retrieved from Myers' rover, but it will take some time to process. Price and Dr. Brooks revealed that their crews opened their rovers once inside the shelter of the cave and took video footage of their own within approximately a mile of the entrance, protected by their oxygenated exosuits. The suits can withstand a good deal, but the decidedly harsh environment in the southern hemisphere would strain even their capacities. However, the cave was surprisingly calm and tranquil, even as howling winds from the dust storm outside were recorded.

From what I've been shown of the footage taken by Myers' rover, the caves are impressive indeed. They are perhaps hundreds of miles long and thousands of feet in height, the ice solid and whitish-blue in color. There are natural formations that appear as if they might have some practical purpose, which is impossible, of course. However, there are cave shelves that are perfectly circular, stalagmites resembling pillars, and even a prominently placed oblong-shaped formation set deep into the caverns.

Myers would likely claim that this is evidence of intelligent subterranean life once existing on the planet. How such life would subsist that far underground is unexplainable, especially with no comestible food sources at hand. Maybe he will have worthwhile ideas to share on this topic—if we ever find him, that is.

Holo-journal log number X67-L98.3

Everyone is saddened at the loss of Myers and the other crew members. They are presumed dead, and another planet-wide dust storm is gathering, most likely even more gigantic and long-lived than the last one. This has made any rescue attempt futile, as traveling over the surface would be impossible under such inclement weather conditions.

Our laser communication system is down; it last worked before the dust storm as we were able to report Price and Dr. Brooks' arrival in the southern hemisphere to headquarters. Now, we're cut off from the company's off-planet network. The communication systems should be up again soon, according to Jacobs (we'll see).

Holo-journal log number X67-L99.6

I've been thinking about some of the things Myers told me about the planet before he left for the southern hemisphere. One is that the planet experienced an extreme ice age within its recent geological past, perhaps ending several hundred thousand years ago. Such a period would correspond to when anatomically modern humans first emerged on Earth.

The ice caverns Myers' crew uncovered could have also formed during that same recent (in geological terms) ice age period. He went on to say that there were likely multiple ice age periods in the planet's geological history spread out over millions of years. This notion agrees with the glacier theory I mentioned in an earlier journal entry.

Back then, the now dry planet would have been solid white instead of red, and there'd have been little light. The conditions would have been more like those of an outer dwarf planet: icy, dark, and far from the sun.

The idea that sentient life—or any life at all, for that matter—had somehow thrived on the planet's surface during this time is unbelievable. It's wrong to speak (or write) poorly of those who have (probably) passed on, but Myers didn't seem to grasp the contradictions in his own thinking, something especially worrisome considering his role as a scientist.

But what sort of life *could* exist under those circumstances, if any? It would have to be well adapted to lightless conditions, able to derive sustenance from difficult or hard-to-imagine sources, and persist even in unimaginably cold environments. Such life, if it could exist at all, would be something utterly alien to our experience.

Holo-journal log number X67-L101

The rover crew maintenance team is close to completing repairs on the two rovers that returned from the southern hemisphere expedition. On top of those two, we have three more held in reserve on our ship. But the dust storm rages on, so no one is leaving our protective dome any time soon.

The lighting in the docking bay where the rovers are housed has been shorting, switching on and off, especially during the night. Dome maintenance says they can't identify the problem, but its source is likely from the electrical interference outside. In any event, the rovers are effectively grounded until this storm passes, whenever that may be.

Holo-journal log number X67-L104.3

Collins is in the medical bay indefinitely, struck down by an unspecified malady or delirium. She told Captain Price that she hears "whispering" in her quarters at night but can't identify what is being said or by whom. The first nights this happened, she blamed on it her overactive imagination, but the strange sounds continued.

Medical Officer Jeffreys has sedated her, but he can only keep Collins under for so long. Collins' panic has reached the point where, just yesterday, she started screaming about escaping from "them" and declaring that "they" were following her everywhere. We can only assume she is an "irrecoverable loss" until the mission is completed and we leave the planet.

Hopefully, something can be done for the poor woman eventually. She may be suffering from something like cabin fever, but we have so little experience with interplanetary colonization that something like her condition has never been recorded before.

Holo-journal log number X67-L108.9

More crew members have come down with the delirium afflicting Collins, including several members of the rover crew maintenance team. All but one of the rover crew is in the medical bay now, sedated due to severe anxiety or even paranoid mania.

Rogers, from the skeleton crew originally stationed at Exploratory Station 3, insisted that our dome is filled with "intruders" who followed the rover teams back from the ice caves. He claims these phantom intruders are watching us from the shadows and are presently waiting for the right moment to strike. Rogers has now been put under as well, leaving us with only one mentally fit driver and rover tech.

As bizarre as the crew members' delusions are, the systems at the base have been acting very strangely. Lights flicker in and out, devices turn on or shut off without warning, and our laser communications system remains offline. The planetary dust storm continues to rage outside, the skies streaked with lightning even in this thin atmosphere. Still, it's difficult to believe that all these odd occurrences could have been caused exclusively by the weather.

Holo-journal log number X67-L111.4

The only rover crew driver not incapacitated, Hughes, opened the docking bay and fled the dome station in a rover earlier today. As there was no one to stop him, Hughes was successful in his escape. He left with no supplies, so it's unclear how long he can expect to survive outside, especially under the ongoing storm conditions.

Of the thirty-three persons at the dome station, less than half are service-ready as of this log entry. Jeffreys has gone violently mad, shrieking about shadowy men, as have others. We have two small holding cells, built as a precaution in case one or two crew members became dangerous, but the cells are woefully insufficient for the present number of deranged crew members.

Those who have been put under sedation are in stasis pods and will remain there until they can somehow be helped. No one is left who knows how to operate the rovers, even Price, but there is nowhere to go on this planet anyway. We are trapped until the dust storm passes and the off-planet communications network becomes operational again.

So, I, too, have begun to hear the whispering voices. At first, it started very subtly, as I slept in my quarters. I would lie in my bed asleep and then awaken suddenly, the sound of someone speaking very softly emanating from the quiet darkness of my room.

Knowing what the others had experienced, I took this at first as a sign I had contracted the delirium suffered by so many of our station crew. I turned on the glow lamps and sat up in my bed, the whispering now gone. I left the lights on, like a child afraid of the dark, but eventually shut them off in an attempt to sleep again. Soon after, as I lay awake, the baleful whispering returned, almost imperceptibly.

I don't believe I'm losing my mind. I'm as steady as before, and my wits are about me. I'm beginning to think that Rogers' ravings may, in fact, contain a grain of truth: something is here with us at the dome station. I'm going to attempt to capture an audio recording of the whispering and see if Jacobs can analyze it. Mercifully, he is still among the sane.

Holo-journal log number X67-L113.6

My handheld audio transcriber shut off in the middle of the night. Whether this was a glitch or an act of our shadowy "friends" is unclear, but I would bet on the latter. I replayed the audio that the transcriber did manage to record and it's nothing but static. It is not known whether the captured audio was noise when initially transcribed.

I'm going to ask Jacobs if I can see the footage taken from the ice caverns. He has been reluctant to share anything about it and has generally been very secretive regarding his investigation. Price and Dr. Brooks have been too preoccupied with the ongoing situation to ask any more about the video and images, presumably not seeing the possible connection to what is now transpiring.

Myers' rover team was able to take hours of video footage before the vehicle stopped relaying images to the rest of the exploratory team's rovers. It's been assumed that the rover crew is dead because no one ever saw or heard anything from them after the relays ceased.

Holo-journal log number X67-L114.2

I spent most of today in the communications room with Jacobs, poring over the video footage. I told him about the whispering, insisting that I wasn't losing my mind, and he seemed to believe me. I asked him what he had found in the footage so far, but he wouldn't answer me.

I asked Jacobs if he had attempted to apply filters to the mostly blurry footage, and he said he had. We went over the list of appropriate filters and descramblers, and I suggested several additional options.

At first, we slowed down the footage in increments until we were close to conducting a frame-by-frame examination, but this revealed nothing important, just as Jacobs had insisted: merely minute close-ups of the ice walls within the incredible network of caverns.

We then sped up the footage, incrementally increasing the frame rate until an hour of footage went by in just minutes. We then applied shading and light filters to the sped-up footage, using them in combination as Jacobs hadn't done before. That's when we finally saw them.

There were thousands of them teeming within the caverns. As the lights of Myers' rover flashed over the cave walls, the tenebrous beings moved aside, as if pained by the bright disturbance. But they were there, skirting the edges of the headlights and moving into the shadows not yet banished.

They appeared like the outlines of people, with limbs and a head, but there were no visible features. Only blackness. They moved so quickly that the naked eye could not perceive them. I think now that they perhaps move in sync with the physical world as we experience it, only much further back and faster.

The full video feed exposed the extent of their society. The cave formations I referenced in an earlier journal entry are their creations, used for unknown purposes. The inhabitants of this planet could have existed for much of its history and clearly still endure. Perhaps they were driven underground by some calamity, or perhaps they evolved down there in the dark.

They are here with us, and we have nowhere to go to escape them. Jacobs' already fragile sanity came close to being broken by the images in the ice caverns; he wanted to destroy the footage, as if that would somehow save us. I argued against this action, saying we had to prove to others that these entities, in fact, exist.

I asked him to show all of this to Captain Price and Dr. Brooks, and he promised that he would. I'm too exhausted and afraid right now to confront them and show them what we have found. I might find the courage to do so tomorrow. I'll just sleep with the lights on tonight. I can't think of anything else I can do to protect myself.

Holo-journal log number X67-L116

I awoke in the night to horrific screaming. It was coming from outside my quarters, further down the hallway. I write this now from inside my locked room. Outside, the screaming continues.

One of the voices sounded like that of Captain Price. The lights in the hall have been put on standby mode, blinking red from what I can see through the transparent duroglass window in my door (I've since closed it).

The generators seem to have failed, and we can't have much power left. The remaining lights will go out first, including those in my rooms, followed by station life support. There is no backup after that.

My hope is that someone will find this log journal and realize the threat humanity now faces. I'll keep it here in my room, hidden in a special compartment familiar to the architects of this dome station. I pray that when help eventually arrives, they find this record and will know what has happened. From there, I hope they might devise a way to overcome the shadow men of Mars.

Matilda Graves

The summer house that Charlotte Evans came to stay in belonged to her father's family. Charlotte's mother never went there, and her father hadn't returned to his family's home for many years. Both were gone, and Charlotte was now alone, an only child. Her aunt on her father's side had offered the place to Charlotte as a means of experiencing a moment of respite before beginning her graduate studies later in the fall.

"I don't like leaving you here by yourself, especially with no way to drive into town," Charlotte's friend, Amelia, reminded her. "I know we've already talked this over, but I still don't like it." Amelia put one of Charlotte's bags on the floor of the house's antiquated kitchen and looked around the compact space. Though the small room was clean and tidy, the kitchen's sink and other fixtures were something from decades past, their surfaces dull and tarnished with age.

"Isolation is what I crave right now," Charlotte said, sighing as she parted the kitchen curtains, rays of sunlight flooding in. "Sometimes, I couldn't even get out of bed after my breakup with Ben. I just need to be alone—no offense." She sat down at the kitchen table and began to rummage through one of the brown paper grocery bags nearby, placed there by Amelia.

Amelia stood by the open door, the pleasant sounds of the woods in early summer ambient in the background. "Will you have enough food for three months?" Amelia asked, frowning as she opened a kitchen cabinet door. Taking out a blue and white box and reading its side, she commented, "I couldn't drink powdered milk. Yuck. I hope you don't starve."

"I'll be fine," Charlotte reassured her, as if dismissing a petulant child. "I think that's all the bags. Thanks for helping me with shopping in town." Charlotte took two cans from the grocery bag and stood next to Amelia, putting them into the cabinet with the powdered milk. "I've got enough food to last until the end of the summer. If I really need to get to town, I can walk. It'll take hours, but I can do it."

"What if you can't walk?" Amelia retorted hastily. "The phone here isn't even hooked up." Amelia leaned against the kitchen counter as Charlotte continued to stash away canned groceries.

"It's a risk I'm willing to take," Charlotte replied. "I'm young and fit. What could possibly happen to me?" She grasped the door to the kitchen and then put an arm around Amelia, hugging her for a moment. "I'll see you in eight-three days. You have a good summer on the water with Ethan. I'm sorry I won't be able to go boating with you two this time."

Charlotte put a hand above her eyes, shading them from the bright afternoon sunlight to watch Amelia drive away. A dirt and gravel driveway led away from the two-story colonial-style house, a paved road then connecting the house to town. A copse of sweeping ash trees hid the house, which stood alone on its own wooded lot with no close neighbors in either direction.

Wandering in the woods behind the house, Charlotte decided to let the rest of the groceries sit in their bags for a while. Everything perishable had already been put away in the refrigerator; Charlotte would have to do without anything fresh once those supplies were gone unless she felt like taking the long walk to town.

The woods were quiet and tranquil, with chirping birds and the soft rustling of leaves in the wind. She strolled along a narrow deer path that eventually opened up into a clearing. In its center stretched a large pond, broad and stagnant, its opposite side lined by dense woods.

Looking out over the pond from its sandy shore, Charlotte noticed how murky the waters appeared. Little sunlight made it to the surface. *It must be very deep at the center*, Charlotte thought, watching the wind churn over the water, tumbling white clouds drifting overhead. *I'll come back later and take another look.*

The old house seemed to breathe as Charlotte walked up its steps, groaning as she opened the front door. *I'm glad Aunt Alice keeps this place in decent shape,* thought Charlotte. *I'll have to visit the elderly couple she employs when I'm in town again, probably in a few weeks.*

The house's attic was cramped, filled with musty furniture, boxes, and a worn steamer trunk, a broken strap dangling from its side. Charlotte had waited until morning to visit the upstairs attic and explore its treasures; she'd been too tired after the long drive with Amelia yesterday.

Opening the trunk, Charlotte began to dig through its contents, putting aside threadbare vintage clothing and leather-bound books. At last, she picked up an old photo album. *I wonder why Aunt Alice doesn't just throw most of this stuff out,* Charlotte asked herself as she turned the dusty pages of the album. *These clothes are just a feast for the moths at this point.*

The photo album held pictures of her extended family from years ago, including people she didn't recognize. Charlotte found photos of her father from when he was a boy and then a young man—he'd grown up in this house before moving away, just like his siblings. The black and white photos were sometimes discolored and there were several empty spaces in the album, as if photos had been taken out.

Putting the book aside, Charlotte took the last of the clothes out of the trunk, something falling out as she did. She reached down to pick up a photo from the floor and examined it. Its picture was of her father standing next to a young, pretty woman. He was smiling. In the background was the house as it would have been many years earlier. Turning the photo over, someone had written "Warren and Matilda" and then marked it with a date.

Looks like Dad had a girlfriend before Mom, Charlotte mused to herself. *I don't remember Mom or Dad ever mentioning a Matilda*. Charlotte tucked the faded, heavily creased photo into the back of the photo album and then tried to put everything back into the trunk in its original order. *I hope Aunt Alice doesn't notice—like she'll even check!*

Rising from the trunk, Charlotte climbed back downstairs to check the mail, closing the attic door above her. *Aunt Alice said I should collect it for her while I'm here.* She opened the front door and walked along the driveway to the sheltering trees and the mailbox hanging from a post near the road. She pried open the mailbox's lid and found nothing inside.

Someone was coming up the road on a bicycle. As the cyclist grew closer, Charlotte could see it was a young woman wearing a summer dress. The young woman waved a hand and then brought her bicycle to a stop near the mailbox, resting her sneakered feet on the pavement.

"Good morning," the woman said gaily, smiling at Charlotte. "It looks like the old place has a guest."

"I'm here for a while," Charlotte replied, returning the woman's smile as best she could. "Housesitting for my aunt, Alice. Nobody lives here anymore, and my aunt wanted the house occupied before it's sold. Are you from town?" Charlotte studied the woman as she waited for an answer. She was naturally beautiful, with flowing, honey-colored hair and striking green eyes. A real knock-out.

"I'm not from town, but I am from around here," the woman answered, still smiling and genial. Charlotte considered this answer somewhat puzzling.

"What's your name?" the woman said.

"Charlotte Evans. Pleased to meet you." Charlotte held out her hand, but the woman only continued to grip her bicycle's handlebars.

"I knew a boy named Evans once. A long time ago," the woman said quietly, her smile fading. She turned away from Charlotte for a moment and looked behind her, as if examining the house.

"And who are you? May I know your name?" Charlotte asked, almost insisting, feeling a sudden discomfort at the break in the conversation.

Without a word, the woman began to pedal off. She didn't turn back or offer an explanation—she just rode silently away. Charlotte watched her glide down the road, her bike bell lightly chiming. Finally, the woman disappeared around a winding curve, gone beyond the leafy trees.

Bewildered, Charlotte returned to the house to make lunch, thinking that she'd pick up again with her summer reading list in the evening. She briefly paused, wondering why a young woman would be riding such an old-fashioned bike.

The fireplace crackled, the only source of light in the living room other than the lamp next to Charlotte's armchair. Charlotte turned a page in her hardback book, nodding for a moment beneath the fireplace's soothing warmth. The night outside was cool; it was still early summer.

When the professor had gone, Sergey Ivanovitch turned to his brother. After reading the first sentence of the new chapter, Charlotte yawned, thinking, *I can't finish this chapter tonight. Maybe tomorrow.*

Resting the book on the side table, Charlotte then heard a floorboard creak upstairs, followed by the sound of soft footsteps. A dull thud echoed from the stairs to the floor below, as if someone had just put their weight onto its steps.

Squinting in the low light of the room, Charlotte glanced cautiously toward the living room's open door. More footsteps echoed in the hallway and then a shadow fell over the entrance. Someone was there—standing in the hall, waiting. Charlotte's lamp light dimmed and flickered, the fireplace's flames dwindling behind her.

"Hello? I know you're there," Charlotte said, now standing in front of her chair. She reached for a fireplace poker and held it firmly, ready to confront her intruder.

There was a mournful sigh and a breeze gushed through the room, its odor fetid and decayed, smelling subtly of fenland. The shadow then receded, pulling back into the dark of the hallway until it finally vanished.

Charlotte hurried toward the light switch on the wall and slapped it on. The ceiling lamp bathed the room in bright light. No one was there.

Poker in hand, Charlotte checked the upstairs bedrooms and then searched the ground floor of the house. Turning on the kitchen lights, she scrutinized the nighttime yard from the front porch and then locked the front and side doors. *I was almost asleep*, Charlotte thought, trying to reassure herself, her uneasiness still palpable. *It was just a dream. I'm all alone out here.*

Charlotte put the house keys into her jeans pocket and then checked her billfold for the cash she had brought with her. *The walk to town will likely take three or more hours*, Charlotte determined. *It's a sunny day, and I can make an excursion of it. But I should've asked Amelia to put her bike in the car trunk for me. I'm just too independent for my own good, I guess.*

She walked to the back of the house, deciding she might find an old bicycle in the house's root cellar. *I haven't looked here*, Charlotte thought as she pulled open its swinging double doors and stepped inside.

The root cellar was dry and lined with jars resting on wooden shelves. Charlotte carefully descended the short set of stairs to the earthen floor and began to search around. The cellar was dark—she could find no suspended light bulb—but the midday sun streaming from the open door supplied enough light.

Against the far wall leaned a rusted bicycle, a wire basket affixed to its front. Standing over the antique bike, Charlotte thought it seemed oddly familiar. It finally came to her: it looked the same as the bicycle of that strange girl she had seen a few weeks ago. Charlotte touched the corroded bell on the left handlebar, finding that it still rang.

This isn't going to get me to town, Charlotte concluded. *I'll just have to walk.* Closing the cellar door behind her, Charlotte joined the road and made a steady pace on foot to her destination. Aunt Alice had given Charlotte the address of the couple who had been keeping her house since last year, asking that Charlotte check in with them at least once during her visit.

When she finally arrived, Charlotte found that the small town was clustered around a charming main street peppered with shops. It ended with a white and gray church, its roof formed into a steeple. Charlotte found a side street that led to several rows of small houses, their exteriors all alike. The elderly couple lived in a cottage past the houses on the town's outskirts.

The cottage was tiny, barely large enough for two people, but quaint and cozy. Charlotte stood on the front steps and knocked on the door.

A withered old woman answered, short and white-haired. "Hello, young lady. How may I help you?" she asked, her smile kindly but vacant.

"I'm Charlotte Evans, Alice Evans' niece," Charlotte replied. "I've been staying at the house these past weeks. Aunt Alice asked me to check in with you once I got settled in."

"Yes, Charlotte. We've been waiting for you. Please come in," the woman said, stepping away from the open door. "Meet my husband, Charles."

An elderly man, stooped and walking stiffly, stopped at the end of the hall. He waved for a moment and then shuffled away, seemingly preoccupied.

"Charles helps me with the house when he can," the woman said, her tone plaintive. "But somedays he's like this. Neither one of us has much time left. But come in."

Stepping inside, Charlotte saw that the home was well kept and pleasantly decorated, with decades' worth of family heirlooms, treasured keepsakes, and portrait photographs filling the living room. The woman slipped into the nearby kitchen and soon returned with porcelain teacups and a teapot resting on a tray. She set the tray on the low table in front of Charlotte.

As the woman poured Charlotte a cup of hot tea, she said, "I'm Iris, by the way. I've known your aunt for many years—she and your father attended school in Winslow. I worked in the school cafeteria, you see. I've lived in Winslow my whole life."

"Pleased to meet you, Iris," Charlotte said, noticing that Charles was now nowhere to be seen. "I hadn't really seen much of Aunt Alice until a few years ago, when Dad passed away."

"Yes, Alice had told us about that. Such a shame," Iris said, her eyes sad. "What about your mother? She was from Winslow as well, you know."

"Mom's gone as well, sometime before Dad," Charlotte replied, her voice full of regret. "But she was taken by a freak accident, not an illness. I always thought I'd see them grow old together, but it wasn't to be."

Iris poured herself a cup of tea and then took a slip. "Your father rarely came back to Winslow after he married your mother," Iris said, her tone becoming steadier. "He lost his first love here, long before her. I suppose that was his reason."

"Who was that?" Charlotte queried, her interest suddenly piqued. "Mom and Dad never talked much about their early years in this small town. I guess they just wanted to forget about it, after moving away and creating a new life for themselves."

"That's a shame, my dear," Iris answered. "When he was a young man, your father loved a girl named Matilda Graves. They were planning to be wed. But, just before the wedding, she vanished, disappeared without a trace.

"People in town said it was cold feet, but I never believed any of it," Iris confided. "Everything she had ever known was in Winslow, and she loved your father more than anything else. Matilda would often talk of the children they would have someday. She's still listed as a missing person, as I understand it."

Charlotte thought back to the photograph she had seen in the attic trunk: her father with a young woman, the name "Matilda" written on its back. Asking quickly, Charlotte said, "Then how did Dad ever meet my mom if he was to be married to someone else? They must have gotten together soon after."

"They did," Iris replied, her answer sharp. "Audrey swooped in, and soon they were dating again. They married shortly after. Your mother had been Warren's steady girlfriend for a while before his engagement to Matilda."

"Well, I don't know what to say," Charlotte said, finishing her cup of tea. "But, like I told you, Mom and Dad seldom discussed their hometown. They were distant, almost absentee, parents in many ways."

There was a silence. Both women peered into their teacups, neither looking at the other.

"Well," Charlotte finally said, breaking the silence, "thank you for the tea. It was lovely. Will you be stopping by sometime this summer?"

"Yes, certainly, my dear," Iris answered, seemingly happy to change the subject. "I'll bring Charles with me if he's able. We drive up to the house. I'm not a young thing like you, you know."

Iris saw Charlotte to the door and waved as the younger woman walked away. Charlotte found her way to Main Street and then the path home. It was late afternoon, and the sun would be setting by the time she arrived back at the house.

The early summer leaves shaded Charlotte as she ambled along the roadside. Her light canvas sneakers were dusty from her long walk and her arm ached from carrying the bag of groceries. Charlotte was tired, surprised that the slow-paced journey to and from town had taken so much out of her. The sun had become burnt orange. It sank slowly below the trees shielding the road from the horizon.

Far ahead in the opposite lane, a bicycle sped toward her. The rider looked like a woman, but Charlotte couldn't quite make her out. The bicycle's bell chimed once and then again, as if warning pedestrians of its arrival. Charlotte turned to follow the rider as she rolled past, finally able to see the woman's face in the dimming light.

The young woman's features were pallid white, like an alabaster death mask. She stared fixedly ahead, not glancing at Charlotte as she rode past; it was as if she was entirely unaware of her presence. The bicycle hastened away, eventually vanishing into the shadows of the first hours of evening.

Shaken, Charlotte thought, *That looked like the girl I met at the mailbox. But she looked . . . strange. Like she was sick.*

As soon as she got home, Charlotte went to sleep, exhausted by her exertions. Tomorrow, she would try to find out more about Matilda Graves.

Charlotte frowned as she studied the picture of her father with the young woman. *It's the same girl,* she thought, *the one I saw at the mailbox on the bike. But it can't be—this picture is decades old.*

Putting the photo away, Charlotte climbed down from the attic to explore the woods behind the house again, hoping to clear her mind. The pond was as she had left it: louring, with scores of lily pads and lines of thin foam floating by its banks.

For the first time, Charlotte noticed a moss-covered rowboat, its oars missing, propped up against a tree not far from the pond. The rowboat seemed as if it hadn't been used for many years, but Charlotte supposed it had probably once taken short trips on the water. The pond was large, after all—almost a small lake.

The wind rustled across the water, causing waves to cascade toward the shore. Charlotte then heard her name on the wind: someone was calling to her. *Charlotte*, the voice whispered, its sound both distant and intimate. Her name again: *Charlotte*. It was a woman's voice, but Charlotte was alone by the water.

Near the pond's unfathomed center, a white shape formed. Slowly, it drifted toward the shore. Charlotte peered ahead, the overcast day offering nothing.

As the shape came closer, it began to rise from the water. First, a head wearing a veil appeared, then a woman's midsection, and finally, wading through the shallows, a woman wearing a full white wedding dress.

The woman moved toward Charlotte steadily, her expression partially concealed by the veil. But, as far as Charlotte could tell, it was unimaginably malevolent.

Charlotte opened her eyes, seeing the star-filled sky above her. The evening was very still, with a bright full moon bathing the grass and leaves nearby with a soft glow. The sky was no longer cloudy as it had been before.

Sitting up, Charlotte realized she was somewhere in the woods, the pond no longer in view. *Where? The water...*

Her head pounding, she stood and peered around. With a wave of relief, she spied the house, its roof jutting distantly through a tangle of trees. Within minutes, Charlotte had reached the front steps and pushed open the door. She heard voices coming from the kitchen.

Charlotte stood at the kitchen's threshold and stared, horror-struck. Two women were seated at the kitchen table, a tea service between them. One was her mother as a young woman and the other was Matilda Graves. They were engaged in a friendly dialogue.

"I'm so glad you could come over to discuss the wedding," Charlotte's mother said amiably. "Warren couldn't be here as he had to help his parents in town. They'll be back tonight."

"I'm pleased, but I'll have to get going soon," Matilda said, "it's still a fair ride back to town on my bike. Warren had a list of things we need to take care of before the big day—did he leave it with you?"

"Why, yes," Charlotte's mother replied, "it's right here. Finish your tea and we'll discuss it." She placed a few sheets of paper in front of Matilda and then excused herself for a moment. When she came back, Matilda complained of feeling drowsy.

"I'm sorry you're not feeling well, dear," Charlotte's mother said, a smile forming on her curved lips. "Perhaps you need to lie down?"

"That's a good idea," Matilda said, nodding. "Just for a moment. Then I'll be fine."

Charlotte's mother helped Matilda to her feet, embracing her with one arm.

"No hard feelings, then?" Matilda asked, pausing to look Charlotte's mother in the face. "You and Warren didn't work out, but we love each other so much. You want him to be happy, don't you?"

Charlotte's mother was silent as the two stood before the kitchen table and then replied, "Of course. That's why Warren will be with me instead."

Matilda grew dizzy and began to swoon, falling against Charlotte's mother. Charlotte's mother pushed her away, letting Matilda fall to the floor with a crash.

Lying on her side, Matilda weakly attempted to grasp something with which to pull herself up. Charlotte's mother stood over her wordlessly and then walked out of the room. She returned with a large trunk sporting thick leather handles.

"You'll fit if I fold you in," Charlotte's mother told Matilda, her words drenched in venom. "But I'm going to take this out to that pond first. Don't go anywhere—not that you can."

The specters faded, and Charlotte heard the ladder to the attic descend with a loud thud. Almost in a trance, Charlotte left the kitchen and stood before the attic's ladder. Slowly, she reached out and began to haul herself up.

The steamer trunk was closed. Charlotte stood by the hatch, unmoving, tears forming in her eyes. Slowly, the trunk's lid began to yawn open. There was a pause—a terrible silence filled the dark space.

A hand shot from the trunk, the fingers distended and claw-like. Charlotte flinched but didn't move. Foul water began to pour from the trunk, forming pools and rivulets around Charlotte's feet.

Matilda rose jerkily, her wedding veil flat against her mottled skin, her eyes bulging, her face bloated and decomposed. Charlotte remained in her spot, paralyzed with fear. She could only watch as Matilda stepped from the trunk and, in slow, loping strides, drew closer. Charlotte could feel the ghost's chill breath on her bare neck.

Matilda leaned in and, in a voice like dead leaves, whispered something in Charlotte's ear.

The sheriff looked down at Iris, who stood next to the attic's ladder below him. She wore a worried expression that changed to one of shock when the sheriff spoke to her: "She's up here, ma'am. She's been dead for at least a few days, given the state of this corpse. I'm coming back down to call the coroner."

Iris stepped aside as the sheriff climbed down. Curtly, he folded the ladder back up and then closed the attic's hatch. "There's no need for you to be here, Mrs. Martin. There's nothing you can do for Miss Evans now. We'll take your statement in town."

Night fell over the empty house, its doors locked and bolted from the outside. The winds rippled over the pond's surface, its waters darkish and foreboding. From within the attic, the sound of sobbing cut through the dark, agonized and afraid. They were coming from the closed steamer trunk, its last memento collected.

About the Author

James Dermond is a writer who lives in Colorado. Intrigued from a very young age by horror anthologies and the short story form, he offers this book as his latest modest contribution to the genre.

Doorways to the Unseen 4: 6 Tales of Terror and Suspense is the fourth volume in a series of short story collections. The fifth volume in the series will be published in October 2022.

To sign up for free eBooks and other future giveaways, please subscribe to James Dermond's author website here:
https://www.jamesdermond.com

James Dermond's Amazon Page
https://www.amazon.com/James-Dermond/e/B01M1S54YP

James Dermond's Goodreads Page
www.goodreads.com/author/show/15862747.James_Dermond

James Dermond on Facebook
https://www.facebook.com/JamesDermondAuthor/

James Dermond on Twitter
https://twitter.com/JamesDermond

Postscript

Thank you for reading this latest volume in the short horror story series, Doorways to the Unseen! We are now on volume four of what will eventually become a twelve-volume series of books. The planned publication schedule is two volumes every year for the next four years, with the final volume released in April 2026. A multi-volume hardcover edition of the collected stories would then be released in October of the same year.

If you enjoyed this collection of stories, please leave a review on Amazon and other online bookstores where volumes in the Doorways to the Unseen series can be found. A positive review will help promote the book and inform other readers of the book's merits.

www.ingramcontent.com/pod-product-compliance
Lightning Source LLC
Chambersburg PA
CBHW020420130626
46549CB00006B/2659